WHO IS BEYOND THE LINE?

"He's right there," she said.

The three of them turned to look where Rachel was pointing. The path of flattened grass Rachel had made led up to a place right next to the Line. On the other side, a similar trodden path approached the same spot.

No one was there.

Ms. Moore walked right up to the Line, the closest she had been to it in years, and spoke. She said she thought she knew what the boy needed to get the medicine across. She told him, or perhaps she only told the meadow, that she would try to get it. She asked him to come back in two nights if he could, to that spot. They all waited to see if he would come out from his hiding place, but there was nothing. Ms. Moore stared into the dark for a long time. Then she turned back to Rachel and Vivian.

"Come to the house with me now. I have some things to tell you."

OTHER BOOKS YOU MAY ENJOY

THE LINE

Teri Hall

Discovery Middle School
Instructional Materials Center
Granger, Indiana

PUFFIN BOOKS
An Imprint of Penguin Group (USA) Inc.

PUFFIN BOOKS
Published by the Penguin Group
Penguin Young Readers Group, 345 Hudson Street, New York, New York 10014, U.S.A.
Penguin Group (Canada), 90 Eglinton Avenue East, Suite 700, Toronto, Ontario, Canada M4P 2Y3
(a division of Pearson Penguin Canada Inc.)
Penguin Books Ltd, 80 Strand, London WC2R 0RL, England
Penguin Ireland, 25 St Stephen's Green, Dublin 2, Ireland (a division of Penguin Books Ltd)
Penguin Group (Australia), 250 Camberwell Road, Camberwell, Victoria 3124, Australia
(a division of Pearson Australia Group Pty Ltd)
Penguin Books India Pvt Ltd, 11 Community Centre, Panchsheel Park, New Delhi - 110 017, India
Penguin Group (NZ), 67 Apollo Drive, Rosedale, Auckland 0632, New Zealand
(a division of Pearson New Zealand Ltd)
Penguin Books (South Africa) (Pty) Ltd, 24 Sturdee Avenue,
Rosebank, Johannesburg 2196, South Africa

Registered Offices: Penguin Books Ltd, 80 Strand, London WC2R 0RL, England

First published in the United States of America by Dial Books,
an imprint of Penguin Group (USA) Inc., 2010
Published by Puffin Books, an division of Penguin Young Readers Group, 2011

3 5 7 9 10 8 6 4 2

THE LIBRARY OF CONGRESS HAS CATALOGED THE DIAL BOOKS EDITION AS FOLLOWS:
Hall, Teri.
The Line / Teri Hall.
p. cm.
Summary: Rachel thinks that she and her mother are safe working for Ms. Moore at her estate
close to the Line, an invisible border of the Unified States, but when Rachel
has an opportunity to Cross into the forbidden zone, she is both frightened and intrigued.
ISBN: 978-0-8037-3466-1 (hc)
[1. Science fiction. 2. Government, Resistance to—Fiction.] I. Title.
PZ7.H14874Li 2010
[Fic]—dc22
2009012301

Puffin Books ISBN 978-0-14-241776-8

Designed by Jennifer Kelly
Text set in Minion

Printed in the United States of America

CHAPTER 1

IT SEEMED TO Rachel that she had always lived on The Property, though this wasn't true. Her mother, Vivian, said they moved there when she was three years old, but Rachel didn't remember. To her, The Property was home. She felt as comfortable there as she did in her own skin. But she knew that for most people, The Property was too close to the section of the National Border Defense System known as the Line.

The National Border Defense System enclosed the entire Unified States. The section called the Line was only a small part of it, but because of its history it was infamous, at least locally. Strange things were supposed to happen near the Line; dangerous things. Even though there hadn't been a Crossing Storm in over forty years, people still thought of the Line as a bad place to be near. There were whispers about Away—the territory on the other side of the Line. There were whispers about the Others.

Rachel wasn't afraid. After all, she spent a lot of her time in the greenhouse that was all the way at the back of The Property, right next to the Line. Away was clearly visible from the greenhouse windows. Rachel had gazed countless hours out those windows at Away, and she had never seen anything strange over there at all. Just the same meadows and trees that were on the U.S. side of the Line.

Technically, Rachel wasn't supposed to be in the greenhouse. Ms. Elizabeth Moore, the owner of The Property, grew orchids there, which she shipped to the cities to sell. Vivian had always cautioned Rachel to stay away from the greenhouse; she worried that Rachel might be a bother to Ms. Moore, or that she might break something. Rachel tried to do whatever she could to make things easier for her mother, but the greenhouse had seemed magical to her from the first time she saw it—so hushed, so peaceful and beautiful. The air was warm and soft, and a gentle light filtered in through the glass, illuminating the lush emerald hues of the orchids' leaves. Their exotic blooms vied for Rachel's attention, some offering flashes of intense colors in bold shapes; others, pale and delicate, coquettishly inviting a closer inspection.

Rachel couldn't resist. She hid somewhere in the greenhouse almost every day when she was little, happy among the flowers. She was careful to stay out of Ms. Moore's sight, of course. She would have been careful even if she hadn't been warned not to bother her. Ms. Moore was old, and not old in a grandmotherly, "here are some cookies" way; she was quite forbidding. Rachel was almost scared of her. But being in the greenhouse was worth the risk.

Rachel used to lose herself there in the kind of daydreams that children who grow up in solitude often have. She'd imagine that she was a princess, the greenhouse was her castle, and the whole of The Property was under her rule. Sometimes she would pretend that she was able to talk with the orchids. Each bloom had a different voice; some were quiet and polite, while others were loud and boisterous. Rachel made them her friends.

Rachel's favorite daydreams when she was a little girl were those in which her father, Daniel, was still alive and had come to take her and her mother somewhere fabulous. In those daydreams, the anxious look Vivian always seemed to wear faded, and she smiled a lot more. Daniel was dashing and handsome, and he let Rachel try things that Vivian would have scowled about, things like climbing tall trees and wandering ahead when they went on walks. In real life, Vivian was always saying "Be careful!" or cautioning Rachel not to stray too far. She looked at Rachel sometimes as though she were waiting for her to break, and that her own heart would break at the same time. But in Rachel's daydreams, if her mother started to protest that Rachel was being too reckless, Daniel would pick Vivian up and twirl her around until she laughed and laughed, and forgot her concern. In her dreams, the three of them could spend every day together, doing whatever they wanted, and Rachel never felt worried.

In actuality, Vivian was busy much of the time working in Ms. Moore's house, where a child underfoot wasn't welcomed. This left Rachel on her own quite a bit, though not completely unsupervised. Ms. Moore's hired man, Jonathan, had helped keep an eye on Rachel when Vivian couldn't. Judging from his grizzled gray hair and his bonsai fingers, twisted from years of arthritis, Jonathan was even older than Ms. Moore. Yet Rachel never felt nervous around him the way she did around his employer.

One of her earliest memories was of Jonathan; she had tripped on something and fallen, and she was crying hard. Her mom must have been working, because it was Jonathan who had gently righted her. She remembered how softly he had said her name and how she felt instantly better. Jonathan always seemed to know how to make her feel safe. He even put up with her playing in the greenhouse, though Vivian didn't approve, as long as she kept out of Ms. Moore's way.

As Rachel grew older, Vivian scheduled enough chores and homework to keep her out of most kinds of trouble, and Jonathan checked in on her less and less. Of course, she wasn't alone all the time. She spent every evening with her mother, and she often rode with Vivian during her weekly supply trips to Bensen, the nearest town. Trips to Bensen, where the highlight might be a treat from the bakery, were about as exciting as things got in Rachel's life. She hadn't minded that when she was little, but as she got older, she often wished that something—*anything*—would happen to her. She loved her mother, and her life on The Property wasn't horrible by any means. But it *was* predictable. Nothing ever seemed to change; no one new ever drove down the long driveway from the main road. There were no other kids to play with, and even though Rachel usually did a pretty good job of entertaining herself, she still got restless sometimes.

Away was Rachel's escape from boredom.

It was inevitable, really. Rachel lived right on the Line. Away was next door, and it was the opposite of boring. It was taboo. Perhaps someone with less imagination, or more friends, could have resisted the pull of something so forbidden, so tantalizingly close at hand, but Rachel was not that person.

Away had been around forever—it was even older than Ms. Moore. Yet it was rarely spoken of, at least officially. The streamer news seldom mentioned it; people in other parts of the country seemed to have forgotten it existed. But the people in Bensen hadn't forgotten. And there was quite a collection of questionable literature about it available on the net. Of course, Rachel read everything she could about Away and the Others, every trashy, "true eyewitness account" she could find.

Vivian would have disapproved if she knew. She had always told Rachel that what happened to the Others was a tragedy, caused by government callousness. She wouldn't have liked the way they were described in Rachel's net books—at best as mindless husks, at worst as monsters. Vivian was pretty strict about Rachel's streamer use anyway; it was reserved mostly for homework assignments. She did let Rachel watch a few stream shows, but only after she had screened them herself.

Vivian wanted Rachel to check out what she called "real books" at the Bensen library when they went to town for supplies. She'd try to talk Rachel into books about art history or girls with pet horses. Rachel thought art history and pet horses were boring and that real books were ancient and smelly. Half of them were falling apart at the seams, and most of the ones she could find about Away were outdated. The graphics were better on the net, and you could find almost anything you wanted, right from the streamer at home.

Rachel would sneak screen time when she was supposed to be doing schoolwork. All the stories about bizarre happenings and weird animals were thrilling. Some claimed that the Others were cannibals, or that they had superhuman strength. One book had outlined the process by which Others could hypnotize a person and enslave them forever, or at least until they wanted to eat them. Even Vivian's protests that the accounts were probably produced by government writers didn't dampen her enthusiasm.

Rachel made up stories in her head about how the Others would creep up to the Line and try with all their might to break through. She imagined seeing one of the odd animals she had read about that were supposed to be so common deep in Away territory, things like birds with funny heads or house cats the size of sheep. Sometimes when she was looking out the greenhouse windows, Rachel *did* see birds on the Away side of the Line, and more than once she had seen deer standing frozen between tree trunks, certain of their own invisibility. But the birds were just regular birds, the same as any bird she'd ever seen, and the deer were just deer.

The Line itself was invisible. There was a barren ribbon of soil running along the meadow as far as the eye could see, where the grass couldn't grow. And Rachel thought she could see a funny sort of haze, but even that was only apparent in certain lights—right before dusk, or early in the morning.

Though the Line was almost imperceptible, it had affected many lives. It affected Rachel's too. In a sense, the Line was the reason Rachel ended up working in the greenhouse, instead of just playing.

Her mom would have said that wasn't true. Rachel could hear the lecture in her head: *It is always a person's own actions that bring about any real change, good or bad.* Vivian would have said a lot more than that if she knew what really happened.

What really happened was that Rachel tried to Cross.

When the U.S. constructed the National Border Defense System, they didn't just ensure that their enemies were kept out. Once the invisible barrier was activated, nobody could leave the country without the government's permission. As far as Rachel could tell, permission was never given to regular citizens; the only people who were allowed to travel outside the borders were political officials or military troops. Crossing—the attempt to leave the country without official permission—was punishable by death.

Trying to Cross would have been bad enough. But Rachel not only tried to Cross, she tried to Cross *the Line*. Nobody *ever* Crossed that section of the System. There was no reason to—there was nothing on the other side but Away.

Rachel had just finished reading yet another net article about Away. In this one, the author described "confirmed" sightings of strange hybrid creatures being commanded by Others, very near the Line. The creatures were supposed to be canine, but as large as horses. The author said they were incredibly beautiful and fierce, and that the Others used them for hunting. The article was dated just two days before. When she saw that, Rachel felt a shiver go down her spine. Two days ago. *Confirmed* sightings. Right in her backyard. Rachel wanted to see those animals. She tried not to think about exactly *what* they might be hunting.

She knew she had to at least *try* to Cross.

She figured there was only a slim chance that she would be able to, since there were only two ways that the System could ever be deactivated. One was a Crossing Storm—a severe electrical storm that was supposed to disarm the System somehow. According to local lore, just such a terrible storm had occurred many years ago, and some Others had managed to Cross somewhere along the Line. Most official records claimed it never happened—the government maintained that there were no verifiable accounts of anything but a terrible weather system that caused some damage. But the local weather reports still called big storms "Crossing Storms." And whenever something bad happened in Bensen—a murder, a break-in, some random vandalism—people blamed the Others for whatever occurred. They whispered that Others were still secretly living among them.

The only other way the System could be deactivated was by the government, if some dignitary had permission to go to another country, or troops needed to Cross. There was no public record of it ever happening on the Line. None of the Crossing Stations from which sections of the System could be disabled were located on the Line. They were all on other parts of the System, the parts where they had had time to plan the construction better. On the Line, the closest thing to a Crossing Station was a little brick bunker near the edge of The Property. As far as Rachel knew, it had always been unmanned; it was locked up all the time and no soldiers ever came to check it. She thought it must be some sort of maintenance shack.

Even though Crossing was likely impossible—or perhaps *because* it was—Rachel worked herself up enough to plan an attempt. She felt like a kid who's been dared to go up to the "haunted" house at the end of some long dark road, only the person daring her was herself. In the back of her mind, she was banking on the probability that nothing would happen. Though she didn't believe most of what she read about the Others in the net books, if even part of it was true, she didn't think she would want to encounter them. *Actually*

Crossing the Line would be the scariest thing Rachel could imagine happening. But the idea of *trying* was exciting.

The next morning, Rachel made the bed and did the breakfast dishes as she waited for Vivian to leave the guest-house where they lived to go work at the main house. Then she put a hunk of cheese and some of the breakfast biscuits in a bag and set out for the back of the greenhouse. If she did somehow Cross, she might need some food.

The day was already pleasantly warm, but Rachel had brought a jacket just in case. She moved cautiously, even though there was no one around. Once she passed the greenhouse, she stopped looking over her shoulder. Nobody could see her this far away from the main house. The closer she got to the Line, the faster her heart pounded in her chest. Everything else seemed eerily quiet.

Finally, she was standing right next to the Line. The meadow grass grew long and shaggy all the way up to where the Line was, but then it died. A line of brown earth about four inches wide extended as far as Rachel could see in either direction. It was different seeing that boundary right at her feet than it was looking at it from the safety of the greenhouse. Away was *right there*, inches from her nose. The only thing separating her from it was the Line. All she could hear was her own breathing, and a sort of rushing sound that filled her head.

Rachel looked hard at the space in front of her, squinting her eyes to see if she could detect how the Line worked, as if something like that has a way of working that you could figure out from staring at it. Her heart thumped so hard it felt like something separate from her.

She forced herself to take a deep breath, then another. The thumping in her chest slowed some. The rushing sound in her head lessened. Finally, she extended her hand tentatively, to see if she could feel the Line, maybe just poke through a little. Her hand was shaking. As she was about to touch the place in midair where she thought it was, there was a shattering sound behind her, so loud it made her jump—*forward*. Into the Line.

It felt sort of like a cloud, or what Rachel imagined a cloud would feel like: soft, but firm against her body, letting her sink into it. But after a moment, it *pushed back*. She was so startled, she fell into the grass. Flat on her back, she gasped for air, while the sky came in and out of focus above her. Then she scrambled up and ran. Her bag of food and jacket forgotten, she fled into the greenhouse, to the safety of its warmth and peace.

Ms. Moore found her there, huddled in a corner crying like a little kid. She had come in to check the orchids and inspect the greenhouse as she did at the start of every day, and soon discovered Rachel's hiding place. Rachel saw Ms. Moore's shoes first; highly polished, brown leather lace-ups of a style that looked like it came from another century. She realized with a growing sense of dread that she was exactly where she had been repeatedly told *not* to be. Ms. Moore, the person who kept food in their bellies, the person Vivian had warned her against upsetting in any way for as long as she could remember, was not looking too pleased. Rachel met her gaze speechlessly and a fresh round of sobs convulsed her.

"I don't have the money to finance your nonsense," said Ms. Moore.

It was the first time Rachel could remember Ms. Moore saying much more than a cursory "Good morning" to her. Rachel didn't understand what she meant about finances, but she knew it couldn't be good. She wiped her eyes and tried to figure out what she should do. She was in big trouble. Her mom would probably kill her. They might be thrown off The Property with no place to go; they might end up living on the street in Bensen. They might even get sent to the Pools. And it would all be Rachel's fault.

Rachel had seen a boy about her age begging for food the last time they went to Bensen. He had on clothes that looked like any other kid's clothes: a jumpsuit and some cheap plastic moks on his feet. But he was so dirty—his face, his hair, even his socks had rings of dirt where they sagged around his ankles. When Rachel asked Vivian about the boy, she just shuddered and hurried Rachel into the vendor's.

"He's still better off than if he was in the Pools," Vivian whispered, once they were inside. "Hopefully he won't get picked up. We're just lucky we found Ms. Moore. At least we have a roof over our heads and the chance of a future." Vivian bought some bread and an apple and gave them to the boy when they came out of the vendor's. He grabbed them without even saying thank you and crammed the bread into his mouth, eyeing Vivian warily the whole time.

Rachel remembered thinking that she never wanted to be that hungry.

"You will have to earn the money to replace that window, young lady."

The words brought Rachel back to the present. Ms. Moore was still looking down at her, shaking her head. The tightly wound bun she always wore—its gray strands so smooth and perfect that they looked more like metal than hair—never moved.

"You can start right now. Get up off your bottom and dry your face. Then go get the hoses from over there." She tilted her head in the direction of the misting equipment hung on the far wall.

Rachel just sat there, stunned into silence and too scared to move. After a moment Ms. Moore, who had begun moving some flowerpots off the main shelves onto the floor, realized Rachel was still crouched in the corner. "Well," she barked, "move it!"

That snapped Rachel out of her freeze, and she scurried up and over to the hoses faster than she had ever moved before. She brought them to Ms. Moore, who took one and hooked it up to a faucet.

"Now, you take the rest and go hook them up to the faucets along that wall. I'll have to go let Jonathan know we'll need a replacement pane for the window you broke." Ms. Moore glared at the floor, and for the first time Rachel noticed the shards of glass she had swept into a pile. Somehow, one of the greenhouse panes had broken. That must have been the shattering sound Rachel heard when she was trying to Cross.

"I didn't break anything." Rachel clamped her mouth shut almost immediately. She didn't want to make Ms. Moore even angrier.

Ms. Moore studied her through narrowed eyes. "Perhaps not. But what you *did* do indicates to me that you need something to fill your time." She nodded at Rachel's shocked look. "That's right. *I saw you.* Messing around out there like you're playing some child's game. That"—she pointed toward the Line—"is *not* a game. That is something…" Ms. Moore's voice shook into silence. When she continued, she spoke so quietly that Rachel had trouble understanding her words. "There's nothing on the other side of that for you, child. Nothing there for any of us. We'll keep what you did between you and me, but best you don't repeat such foolishness. You'd better go get your coat before someone else sees it there."

Rachel mumbled an apology, but Ms. Moore just turned and left. Rachel watched her walk toward the main house. She wondered why just *talking* about Away caused Ms. Moore's voice to shake like that. Rachel knew that all the stories she read about Away and the Others were probably not true. But what *was* true?

She picked up one of the hoses, but then put it back down. Before she hooked them up, she had better go get her jacket like Ms. Moore said. On her way out the greenhouse door she looked toward the main house, but Ms. Moore was gone from sight.

Ms. Moore knew *something*, Rachel could tell. She'd lived right next to the Line her whole life, according to Vivian. In all that time, maybe she had found out something about Away, something about the Others. Rachel decided then and there that she was going to find out what.

That evening, Rachel had done all her homework, cleaned the guesthouse, and made dinner. She waited with dread for Vivian to come back from the main house. By the time Vivian walked in the door, one look from her was all it took to make Rachel burst into tears again. She had never done anything to truly disappoint her mom before, and she could see in her eyes that Vivian was disappointed now.

Vivian came over and put her hand on Rachel's head, smoothing her hair. Then she hugged her. "Oh, Rachel. Probably just having to work with Ms. Moore will be punishment enough for you," she said. "She's not always the easiest person to be around. And you're going to be around her a lot for the next three months."

"Three months!" Rachel couldn't fathom what three months of seeing Ms. Moore every day might be like.

"That's how long it will take to earn enough to pay off that window." Vivian gave Rachel a look that clearly conveyed her standard "learn from your mistakes" lecture in one glance. "Mind you do what she tells you and work hard. No matter how gruff she seems. We *cannot* afford to upset her. Jonathan will be there, and that will help."

Despite Vivian's hug and her comforting words, Rachel knew the seriousness of what she had done. If Ms. Moore had been angry enough to fire Vivian, they might have had no choice but to go back to the city. Rachel knew her mom didn't want to do that. She didn't want to either. Things could be really bad in the cities.

ELIZABETH MOORE ADDED the cost of a new window to the expenditures column of her old-fashioned account book and closed it. It would have to be one of the new plastic windows; they didn't manufacture glass anymore. Elizabeth resented that for no good reason. The plastic ones worked just as well, probably better, but the glass windows had been there so long that they felt like a tradition—not something to be abandoned due to mere obsolescence. She'd had to replace two others last year. The glass just got so old and brittle, it shattered spontaneously. She was sure that was what had happened today as well, but she accused the girl anyway. Because when she saw Rachel by the Line, she knew that it would be best to keep a closer eye on her from now on. One way to do that was to make her work in the greenhouse.

She smoothed the wood grain of the dining table with her hand. Real mahogany. It was at this same table that she had interviewed Ms. Vivian Quillen, Rachel's mother, so many years ago, for the position of housekeeper. Ms. Quillen was in some sort of trouble back then, Elizabeth could tell; she had some experience in that area. The haunted look on Ms. Quillen's face had made Elizabeth want to bid her good day, even though she was the only person who had responded to the ad. Elizabeth could do without help for the time being. Then Ms. Quillen mentioned the child. That complicated things.

There hadn't been a child on The Property since _Elizabeth_ was that child, running in the yard, laughing at the sky. And being reminded daily that children even existed was not something Elizabeth really wanted to endure; it was painful. Yet turning away a grown woman who was capable of finding alternatives was a different thing than turning away a mother and child, who might not have a better option. Elizabeth had not wanted to be responsible for the possible consequences. So she had hired the woman, against her better judgment.

She wondered if she was going to pay for that now. Maybe whatever led the mother to trouble had been passed on to her daughter, causing her to seek out trouble as well. Elizabeth hoped that by keeping Rachel busy working in the greenhouse, she could steer her away from her interest in the Line. And it might solve other problems too. Jonathan had his hands full, and while Elizabeth was sure he would have tried to help, he didn't have the touch. As her father always said, "Orchids aren't potatoes." What he meant, and what Elizabeth had always believed, was that to grow beautiful, healthy orchids, one could not view them as a crop. A part of you had to love them, be in love, to grow them well. Elizabeth had that feeling. She thought Rachel might have that feeling too, judging from how much time the girl had spent in the greenhouse over the years.

CHAPTER 2

Rachel was more than a little apprehensive about working for Ms. Moore. In all the years Vivian and Rachel had lived on The Property, the lady had never once relaxed her formality. She was always Ms. Moore—never Elizabeth—even to Jonathan, who had known her forever as far as Rachel could tell. She never asked about their lives outside the work they did for her, and she did not encourage questions about her own.

Vivian had told Rachel that when she first started working for Ms. Moore, she'd made the mistake of commenting on a framed digim she saw on the mantel in the main house, where she was dusting.

"Oh, Ms. Moore," she had said, "is this a picture of your husband? He was a fine-looking man."

Vivian said the silence had been stunning, like being doused with ice water. She turned to look at Ms. Moore, who was staring at her as though she had discovered a dead rat in her parlor.

"I," said Ms. Moore, slowly and distinctly, "was never married." She looked at Vivian for a moment more, as though she were trying to decide exactly how one would dispose of such an unpleasant object without actually having to touch it. Then she walked away.

On her way out, without turning her perfectly coiffed head, she said, "I prefer to keep my personal life *personal*, Ms. Quillen. Please start in the kitchen next."

Vivian usually laughed when she told that story, but Rachel didn't think it was so funny now that *she* was going to have to work for Ms. Moore.

AS IT TURNED out, Rachel learned most of the daily routine in the greenhouse from Jonathan. Ms. Moore was there the first morning, but she said little. She handed Rachel a thick, plastic-covered notebook filled with printouts and told her to study it. "There are specific ways to behave around orchids, Rachel, and you will need to learn them if you are to be allowed to work here. Jonathan will instruct you in the simpler tasks and inform me of your progress." With that, she left.

Rachel's expression must have been quite forlorn, because Jonathan smiled down at her and winked. "Now, child, she's not so bad," he said. "Just has no use for the pleasantries in life. At least not anymore." He looked at the doorway Ms. Moore had disappeared through, far away for a moment.

"Did she used to be different?"

"Hmm?" Jonathan looked back down at Rachel.

"You said 'not anymore.' Like she used to be different." Rachel thought about that. "My mother used to be different, before."

"Before what?"

"Before my father died."

Jonathan cocked his head at her. "How do you know, dear? You've been here since you were tiny. How would you remember she was different?"

"We have digims of him," Rachel said. "When she looks at them . . . she shines. That's how she must have been before." Rachel searched Jonathan's eyes, certain he wouldn't know what she meant. She was surprised when he nodded.

"It takes something—important—away," Jonathan said. He looked thoughtful.

"What does?" Rachel wasn't certain what he meant.

"Losing love." Jonathan smiled, but he didn't look happy. "Especially that kind of love."

"Do you know about that?" Rachel looked away as soon as she said it. It was a very personal thing to ask, and she thought she had a better chance of getting an answer if she wasn't watching Jonathan's face. She kept her eyes on the notebook Ms. Moore had given her.

Jonathan said nothing for a time. Rachel was certain he wasn't going to reply, when he finally did.

"I think we all know a bit about that, here on The Property. All of us but you, my dear. And I hope you never learn." He cleared his throat, as though something was stuck in it. "Let's get started with the misting, shall we? I know how to do most of the regular chores the flowers need done, though I'm sure *she* might not agree. The rest you're to learn from those notes." Jonathan patted her shoulder and began to show her the morning routine.

THREE HOURS LATER the misting and feeding were done, and Jonathan had left her to go take care of some of his own work. Rachel was sitting on a stool in front of one of the workbenches, staring at a particularly beautiful, garnet-colored bloom without seeing it. She had been thinking about what Jonathan had said about love. About how losing it took something away.

She was glad she didn't have to worry about it. A few times lately, Vivian had tried to talk with her about "adult" love. Rachel giggled, thinking of it. That was what she had called it—*adult love*. Vivian couldn't figure out why Rachel giggled so much every time she brought it up. Rachel didn't tell her there was a stream show called *Adult Love*. She had accidentally seen a brief glimpse of a scene before clicking away from it out of sheer embarrassment. She was pretty certain what she had seen was not the same thing Vivian meant. Vivian never got too far with whatever it was that she *did* mean, because Rachel just scoffed.

"Mom," she had said. "Look around. Do you see any people besides you and me and Ms. Moore and Jonathan?

Who exactly am I in danger of falling in love with? Besides, I'm just not interested."

"Someday you will be, Rachel." Vivian had looked worried.

Rachel had just shrugged. "Well, we can talk about it then, okay?"

RACHEL STUDIED THE printouts Ms. Moore had given her every evening after her regular schoolwork was done, and quickly became captivated by what she was learning. Of course, she had always appreciated the orchids' strange beauty. She was mesmerized by the butterfly blooms of the phalaenopsis, the spray of delicate wings arching skyward. She was drawn in every time by the heavy, spicy richness of the cattleya, with its drooping, jewel-toned petals. Even the odd, almost ugly flowers of some of the catasetum fascinated her.

But orchids had secrets, too, and Rachel was learning them. As she studied each evening, she found herself fascinated by their oddities. Some orchids could live in almost any circumstances, while others required such particular conditions in order to propagate, it seemed impossible that they survived at all. Some fed from the very air; others trapped their food or fooled insects into pollinating them. Many were breathtakingly gorgeous, but there were orchids that looked more like creatures than flowers. There was one orchid—*Dracula tubeana*—that looked exactly like a bat.

Ms. Moore checked on Rachel's progress once a week, watching while Rachel carried out the daily tasks required to keep the orchids growing and healthy. She commented on what Rachel was doing, quizzed her about the particular variety she was misting or feeding.

"Why are you giving the phals that mix?" Ms. Moore, perched on a stool, watched Rachel as she worked.

"It's to help with bloom strength," said Rachel. "This fertilizer has a higher phosphorus content, and that helps the flowering process."

Ms. Moore looked pleased. "Correct. Now, let's move on to how one would repot those dendrobiums." Ms. Moore indicated several pots of orchids sitting on the workbench. Their roots were creeping up over the lips of the pots, seeking out new territory to conquer. "Tell me the steps."

"First, I would carefully remove the plant and medium from the pot. Then I would very gently get all of the old potting medium off the plant's roots." Rachel looked at Ms. Moore to see if she was right so far.

"Go on."

"Then I would check the roots for any damage or disease. I would check the leaves too."

"And what are you looking for when you check the roots?"

Rachel thought about the notes she had studied the night before. "Soft spots. Or roots that are all dried up?"

"And if you find that?"

"I would remove those roots from the plant." Rachel bit

her lip. There was something more . . . and then she remembered. "I have to sterilize the scissors. Because orchids can get infections and so all the cuts have to be sterile."

Ms. Moore nodded. "Very good, Rachel. You've got a lot more to learn, but you are doing well."

"Should I repot these?" Rachel pointed to the dendrobiums.

"That's why they're here. I'll observe."

Rachel picked up the nearest pot and got to work. For a few minutes there was silence while she brushed dusty potting medium off the roots of the first plant. As she became less nervous about her task, Rachel decided to take a risk.

"Ms. Moore?" Rachel kept her eyes on her work.

"Yes, Rachel?"

"Um." Rachel wasn't sure how she should start. "How do you like, um, how do you like living here?"

"Careful with that leaf." One of the leaves on the dendrobium was being bent too far because of the way Rachel was holding it.

"Oh." Rachel adjusted her grip.

"By 'here' I assume you mean The Property?" Ms. Moore looked at Rachel quizzically. "Not *here* near the town of Bensen, or *here* in the Unified States?"

Rachel nodded.

"I like living here just fine." Ms. Moore's reply rang with a certain finality, as if there were nothing more to add to the subject.

"Why do we call it *The Property*?" Rachel realized as she asked the question that she had never wondered about it before. "They don't call it that in Bensen." She had heard a vendor ask her mother once, in a half whisper, how it was to work "out there on the Moore place."

"We just always have." Ms. Moore sounded quite piqued that Rachel was still asking questions, but she continued. "Long ago that's all it was—a piece of property. There was no greenhouse, no business, no home. I imagine my grandfather had lots of conversations with my grandmother about 'the property,' about his dreams for it, his hopes." For a moment Ms. Moore seemed as though she might share something more, but the moment passed.

"That one is done. On to the next." Ms. Moore gestured to the row of pots waiting on the workbench.

Rachel untangled the roots of the next dendrobium from the drainage hole of its pot. It took her a few moments, but she gathered the courage to press on with her investigation.

"So, have you ever noticed anything . . . strange happening here?" She snuck a quick look at Ms. Moore. "Anything odd, or, um . . ." Rachel's voice trailed off into nothingness. She risked another glance at Ms. Moore, and sure enough, the lady was regarding her with a quizzical look, head tilted to one side.

Ms. Moore kept looking at Rachel for what seemed like a very long time. Then she turned her attention to the dendrobium Rachel was holding.

"Do you see how that root is all dark and wilted? That one definitely needs to be trimmed."

That was as far as Rachel progressed in her quest for information, at least on that day. She could tell by Ms. Moore's demeanor that more questions would not be well received. She wasn't going to give up though. After all, Ms. Moore couldn't have lived so close to the Line for so many years without knowing *something*.

CHAPTER 3

RACHEL AND HER mother had come to The Property after Rachel's father was lost in the last war between the Unified States and Samarik. Rachel had researched it; she wanted to know what her father had died for. Vivian would never say much about it, but according to the net archives, Samarik claimed the U.S. was engaging in "cruel and inhuman" practices. Things like apprehending citizens and forcing them to work in government Labor Pools if they couldn't pay random taxes. Samarik believed that citizens deserved public trials and reasonable sentences. The U.S. wanted Samarik to stay out of their affairs, and they sent troops to make sure the message was clear. The U.S. won, of course, but a lot of fathers died winning. When Rachel's father was reported as a casualty, Vivian was left to figure out how to support the two of them.

Rachel was little then, so she didn't have any memories of it, but Vivian had told her many times the story of how she found The Property. Vivian kept a printout of the ad that Ms. Moore had placed in the Domestics section of the daily classifieds—a torn scrap of yellowing paper—tucked in her brown leather portfolio. The portfolio was where she kept things that were important to her: things like birth certificates and letters, and digims of them—Vivian, Rachel, and Daniel—when they were still a family.

Rachel's favorite digim was of the three of them standing in a room that looked about as big as Ms. Moore's linen closet. Vivian was beaming, more carefree than Rachel had ever seen her look. Daniel was holding Rachel—a tiny baby at the time—and smiling. He had thick brown hair, which Vivian said was exactly like Rachel's. He looked nice. Rachel didn't remember him at all.

When Vivian looked at that digim, her eyes would glow for a moment. That's how Rachel thought of it—that they glowed. But the glow would soon fade, replaced by the sadness that Rachel was used to seeing. She was so used to that sadness she hadn't realized that was what it was for the longest time. It had just always been there, a part of Vivian, like the tiny scar on her chin or the bump on her nose. Once, Rachel had found her mother holding that digim, crying. When Vivian realized she was watching, she had quickly dried her tears and smiled at Rachel. "It's okay, honey," she had said. "I still have you."

Rachel tried hard to be enough. She rarely disobeyed Vivian, and she always did her chores around the guesthouse. She had even begun to learn to cook, so she could make dinner sometimes. Still, she didn't think there was anything she could do to make the sadness in her mother's eyes disappear. And though she only had stream shows to use as comparisons, she didn't think that most mothers looked at their children as though they were afraid they were going to break. Still, Vivian didn't *always* act sad. In fact, most of the time Rachel couldn't imagine a better mother.

They were their own little family, with their own unique family history. Like the story of how they came to live on The Property. Retelling that story was one of their rituals; one of the things they did together, like some families retell "How I Met Your Father" stories.

"I was at my wits' end," Vivian would say, when she was feeling particularly safe and secure. Those were the times when she took a moment to relax. She usually only did that on holidays, her work for Ms. Moore temporarily done, the few holiday bonus creds she earned safely transferred to Rachel's education account. She had time then to take a long, warm bath, or enjoy a glass of wine. Then she would snuggle into the old afghan on the couch, pat the spot next to her to invite Rachel to come snuggle too, and tell her the story about coming to The Property.

"I had no idea how we were going to eat the next day," she would say, "let alone pay the rent, which was a week and a half overdue. I was so afraid, Rachel. It seemed like I had been desperate for so long, though it had been only a few days since I got the letter about your dad."

Rachel had seen that letter too. It was in the portfolio

along with the rest of the memories Vivian kept. It wasn't a printout of a netcomm. It was a real letter, which looked very official, with the blue U.S. seal impressed into the paper. It still said her father was dead no matter how many times Rachel read it.

"What did you do, Mom?" Rachel didn't need to ask; she knew the story by heart. But there was something about the ceremony of it, snuggling together on the couch, asking the same questions, hearing the same answers, that comforted her. She thought it comforted Vivian, too.

"I was looking in the Domestics section for jobs, since I didn't really have any other skills." Vivian ruffled Rachel's hair. "When you go to college, we're going to be sure you take more than art history classes. And that you get your degree *before* you fall in love with some man and marry him." She laughed.

Rachel smiled, but she said nothing. She wasn't going to fall in love. If love took the light from your eyes, the way it had from Vivian's, Rachel wanted nothing to do with it.

"I thought I could clean and do shopping for someone. So the Domestics section it was. The ads all wanted someone to come in once a week, maybe twice a week, but that wouldn't work for us. I had nobody to leave you with, and none of those jobs paid enough to cover a place of our own anyway. I was sure I would have to register for the general Labor Pool. We would have ended up in a community residence. Oh, Rachel. When I think of what could have happened! Then I saw Ms. Moore's ad."

This was the place in the story where Vivian always took out the printout, unfolding it and smoothing its wrinkled surface carefully. It looked like this:

LIVE-IN HELP REQUIRED

Domestic for cleaning, meals, errands, and laundry. Private quarters, board provided, small monthly compensation. Must be hard-working, polite, and neat. No college students need apply. Contact Ms. Elizabeth Moore, 1218 West Meeky Road, vocall 48912706. Interviews will be held Tuesday, September 10, between 1 p.m. and 4 p.m.

"I was a bit nervous about the job being so far away from anything. I mean, we're practically in the middle of nowhere," said Vivian. "But once I actually saw the place, it looked perfect—way out here where nobody would bother us. I knew we would be safe here."

Rachel thought she knew what her mom meant. It was good to be out in the country. Things weren't so great anywhere in the U.S., but the cities were the worst, especially since the government passed the New Rights Bill.

The New Rights Bill was, according to Vivian, a travesty. Rachel agreed, since she had actually seen a copy of the old bill, the original one from before all the new amendments were added. Rachel didn't know why Vivian had a copy; possessing one became a crime once the New

Rights Bill went into effect. It was not kept in the portfolio. Too dangerous, according to Vivian, and she wouldn't tell Rachel where she kept it. But she did show it to Rachel one evening during their lessons. She went over each line, explaining how the original bill protected the people and kept the government from doing anything too bad. She told Rachel how the government kept adding new amendments and how they finally scrapped the whole thing, replacing it with the New Rights Bill. Vivian always called it the *No Rights Bill.*

Now the government could do pretty much what they wanted, and sometimes what they wanted was not so nice. Rachel and Vivian were lucky, because living on The Property, they didn't have to deal with most of the things that happened in the cities. Things like Identifications, or getting charged with a random tax and not having the creds to pay it. The government stopped collecting random taxes in rural areas when they stopped the road maintenance, but in the cities people were Identified all the time, hauled away for nonpayment or some other unexplained infraction, held until they came up with creds for the fine. If they couldn't pay, they were sent to a Labor Pool.

Everyone was in the Identification System, of course; individual genids were recorded at birth, so if someone's name was flagged in the system and the government wanted to Identify that person, they could, even out in the rural areas. But it probably cost more for Enforcement Officers to come out to places like The Property to claim someone than they could collect in fines. Mostly they didn't bother.

THE GUESTHOUSE WAS small, but it was warm in the winter and the rent was part of Vivian's salary. There was a tiny front room and an area off to one side of it that served as a kitchen. Vivian and Rachel shared the bedroom, and they had a little garden in the side yard where they raised their own vegetables. Vivian brought some things with her when they came, but not much. There was a woolly crocheted throw for the couch and an old-fashioned reading lamp, almost as old-fashioned as the stuff in Ms. Moore's house. It had a real glass shade that was the same color as the daffodils that sprouted in the yard every spring. It sat on a little table next to the couch, where they read to each other at night, when Vivian wasn't too tired. Sometimes Vivian ended up snoozing in front of the streamer. Rachel thought she worked too hard. She wished she could help in more ways than she did, but she wasn't sure what else she could do.

Until she started in the greenhouse, the only work Rachel did besides her regular chores was to study for the tests Vivian gave her as a part of her homeschooling. After a brief experience at the Bensen Council School, Vivian decided Rachel would be better off learning what she could teach her at home. Rachel barely remembered attending the Bensen School, only flashes of too many people and lots of other kids and how mean the teacher looked. One of her first homework assignments was to write a paper outlining how the New Rights Bill benefited the citizens of the Unified States. When Vivian saw that she pulled Rachel out of school.

Vivian tried as hard as she could to get accurate information for Rachel to study, but it was difficult. She used library texts and printouts from streamer sites for lessons, but those were usually scrubbed pretty clean of the truth. She filled in information where she could, and she and Rachel had a lot of discussions about how the materials available were edited to show the government in a positive light.

"You can't always believe what you're told, Rachel," she would say. "Whenever you watch streamer coverage about some issue, remember who controls the media."

Rachel wondered how Vivian thought she could forget, the way she repeated that over and over. Sometimes Rachel would stare straight ahead and in the most robotic voice she could come up with she would chant, "The government controls the media, the government controls the media," until she couldn't help but laugh. Most of the time, Vivian laughed too. But she *always* said, "Remember that."

Vivian wanted Rachel to attend a private college when the time came, one that didn't teach what she called "the party line." But she also told Rachel that with their lack of connections, *any* college would do. If Rachel could get into a college, she could register for a Profession, and that was all that really mattered to Vivian. Rachel didn't see where she had much choice; the alternatives to a Profession were pretty grim. Vivian made her study the political and social systems in the Unified States as a part of her home lessons, so she knew what the options were.

There were limited choices for people in the Unified States: a Profession, Private Enterprise, Gainful Employment, or the Labor Pools. People in the Professions—doctors, attorneys, engineers and other highly skilled occupations—had to pay high taxes, but they were insulated from the worst of the governmental intrusions and lived comfortable lives as long as they conformed to the rules. Her father had been registered in a Profession as an architect. She thought that might be as interesting as anything.

Private Enterprise, which was what Ms. Moore did in her orchid business, was more and more difficult to succeed at because of all the tariffs and regulations the government enforced. People who couldn't afford college made a go of Private Enterprise if they could, because the only other choice was Gainful Employment, which was precarious. If a person lost their job, they had a limited time to get another one. If they couldn't find one fast, they were sent to the Labor Pools. That had been Vivian's greatest fear before she found Gainful Employment with Ms. Moore. The Labor Pools were not where anyone wanted to find themselves.

People also ended up in a Pool because they couldn't come up with the creds to cover a random tax, or sometimes because the government wanted them to disappear, though those people usually disappeared in a more permanent way, if the rumors were accurate.

Poolers lived in "community residences," a fancy term for barracks, and worked for room and board. The one perk they had was that they were given generous reproduction licenses, because their children were basically a renewable government resource. Pooler kids were registered into Labor Pools on the day they were born, trained from toddlers to become grid maintenance workers, or highway or computer techs; whatever the projections showed there would be need for in the coming decades.

Vivian swore that Rachel wouldn't end up in a Labor Pool no matter what, and college was the only sure way to prevent that from happening. Vivian saved every cred she could toward tuition, and she put together pretty tough course work for Rachel to master in the meantime. Rachel got so tired of the lessons sometimes.

Still, she knew Vivian was doing it for her own good. She also knew that it all had something to do with her mother's fears, with the idea that if anything happened to Rachel, life would not be worth living. So Rachel did her best to apply herself to her schoolwork. She didn't want to add to Vivian's sadness. And to be truthful, the idea of ending up in a Labor Pool was frightening. She didn't know much about them; just the way her mother said the words was scary enough.

CHAPTER 4

"Oh, Rachel," Vivian said. "Not again." She had just come from the main house, finished with work and ready to review Rachel's homework before dinner.

Rachel looked up guiltily from where she sat in front of the streamer. She had been reading another article about Away. "What?"

"You know very well what, young lady." Vivian shook her head. "If you think I don't know what your reading habits are when I'm not looking, think again." Vivian crossed the room and glanced at the streamer screen. "More nonsense about Away, I see." She flicked off the streamer.

Rachel said nothing. She knew better than to protest.

"I think before dinner, it's quiz time," Vivian said.

"But I've got dinner all ready to go," Rachel said, hoping Vivian would let her off easy. She *hated* quizzes. "It just needs a few minutes to warm up and we can eat."

"That was so *thoughtful* of you, dear. We can use that

few minutes for our quiz." Vivian tilted her head at Rachel. "Hmm. Since you're so fascinated by Away, let's review how it actually came to be. Starting from the Deactivation Acts and the Global Weapons Accord."

Rachel groaned. So much for getting off easy. "Mom, those were *way* before Away. The National Border Defense System wasn't even built yet."

Vivian just looked at her. "What were they designed to do?"

Rachel hung her head. "They were designed to limit the destruction of war. Wars were becoming too damaging. The weapons used had the potential to destroy the earth. Certain types of weapons were prohibited."

"Were the limitations effective?"

"Well, that depends on what you mean by effective. We probably won't destroy the planet, but we still have wars." Rachel shrugged.

"So they were effective, in the way they were *designed* to be effective," Vivian said. "Because none of them was ever meant to *stop* war. They were meant to stop us from incinerating the planet, just as you said, Rachel." Vivian scowled. "I don't know that most governments really *want* to stop war—it has too many uses. But that's another day's lesson."

The timer dinged, indicating that their dinner was ready.

"Thank goodness." Rachel hopped up and started toward their small table, which she had set with dishes.

"Not so fast," Vivian said. "We can quiz and eat at the

same time." She brought the food to the table. Rachel groaned again.

"Okay." Vivian poured water from the pitcher for each of them, ignoring Rachel's protest. "So what effect did the Deactivation Acts have on warfare?"

"War tactics changed." Rachel was glad she had studied the night before. "When high-tech weapons were banned, countries had to fight in more old-fashioned ways. Troops, heavy artillery, direct physical attacks on borders." Rachel served herself a piece of corn bread and passed the rest to her mom.

"Thank you, dear. This looks delicious."

"What does any of the Deactivation stuff have to do with Away?" Rachel didn't remember anything about Away in the reading her mom had assigned. It had all been about long-ago political accords and pacts.

"I'm getting there," Vivian said. "The change in fighting techniques leads us to the National Border Defense System. Why was that constructed? Wait, two-part question. (A) why was it constructed, and (B) why was it controversial?"

Rachel grinned. "I know this. (A) it was constructed because with the change in fighting techniques, a physical border protection system was the best way to defend us from ground invasion. (B) . . . um . . . it was controversial because even though most other countries already had one long before the U.S. built ours, the U.S. had always upheld individual freedom as a right. If they built the National Border Defense System, people wouldn't be able to just come and go from the country. The government said the type of system they were going to build was different than the ones most other countries had—that it was super-special or something—and that it wouldn't be easy to disarm. They were restricting the borders. So there was a lot of protest about that."

"Hmm." Vivian thought for a moment. "Well, on (A), you got it mostly right. It was the most *economical* way to protect the borders from invasion. That doesn't mean it was the best. And as for (B), yes. The U.S. was based on individual freedoms being our right. At least at one time. And people didn't want their right to leave the country removed." Vivian smiled at Rachel. "Somebody *did* do their reading assignment, even if all those net books seem so much more enticing."

"I always do my assignments, Mom." Rachel looked up from her plate and saw Vivian's expression. "Well, almost always."

"So, now we're getting to what the National Border Defense System has to do with Away." Vivian took a sip of her water. "Even though there were protests about the System, it was built anyway, right? So tell me what building the System has to do with Away."

Rachel pointed to her mouth; she had just taken a bite of corn bread.

"I get it now," she said, once she could speak again. "The Korusal threat, the whole rush construction job on the Line."

"Exactly!" Vivian nodded. "Come on. You don't get off that easily; I want the history lesson here."

"Korusal was about to attack the U.S.," said Rachel. "They were huge back then, but we had more advanced technology and they wanted it. So they were going to launch an attack, but somehow word got out. The U.S. only had a small section of the System left to finish, but it involved some complicated shoreline work. They didn't think they had time to do it before Korusal attacked. So the U.S. was worried because, with the number of ground troops they had, Korusal could have really done some damage if they got in where the border was unprotected. The U.S. and Unifolle had an emergency meeting—"

"Why Unifolle?"

"The U.S. figured they could close their border system in time to stop the attack if they just built in a straight line to Unifolle's system, where it shared their border. And that's what they did. Without any real notice to people. So lots of people got stuck outside when they activated the System. And when Korusal attacked, the unprotected area—what is now Away—got blasted. To make it worse, Korusal used prohibited weapons, or at least that's the claim. I don't think they ever proved that, did they?"

Vivian shook her head. "No, they didn't ever prove it, officially. And nobody has had any real information about Away for decades. But they got really strange readings from that area for years after the blast." She wiped the table off and tossed the cloth in the sink. "And all of your exaggerated net book stories are based on those strange readings and some unsubstantiated rumors about the Others."

"They can't all be completely wrong." Rachel turned her head so that Vivian wouldn't see her grin. "After all, even the streamer news shows have stories about the Others—weird stuff they might be responsible for and possible sightings."

"But that's my point, Rachel," Vivian began, sputtering with frustration. "The official story—"

"Isn't always the true story." Rachel laughed. "I know, I know. I'm just teasing you."

"You . . . *brat*." Vivian charged at Rachel, who ran, giggling. Vivian chased her around the couch until they were both breathless.

"Truce!" Rachel held up her hands.

"Okay, truce." Vivian collapsed on the couch, breathing hard.

Rachel flopped down next to her.

"Mom, what do you really think happened to them? The people who got stuck Away, I mean. The Others."

Vivian shrugged. "What makes you think anything happened to them? Besides being shamelessly abandoned by their own country and left to fend for themselves in a war zone? Oh, and then banished forever because of some lie about national security breaches and unknown contamination factors. Let's not forget that." Vivian snorted.

"Is that really the only reason they won't let them back in? Do you really think all the stories are just . . . stories?"

"Who really knows, Rachel." Vivian ruffled Rachel's hair. She sounded tired. "Well, I think I'm off to bed. You coming soon?"

"Pretty soon. I have to go over some notes from Ms. Moore for tomorrow. She's going to let me try pollination." Ms. Moore had demonstrated the technique twice now and explained how it could create a whole new kind of orchid depending on what two species were crossed. The idea of creating an entirely new thing, something that had never existed before she made it, was extraordinary to Rachel. Ms. Moore had cautioned her that hybrids, or crosses as Ms. Moore called them, could take years and years to bloom. Some would never bloom at all. But that didn't bother Rachel. She was intrigued by the possibility—the possibility of what might become.

CHAPTER 5

Dᴜʀɪɴɢ Rᴀᴄʜᴇʟ's ᴛʜɪʀᴅ month working in the greenhouse, the last she was obligated to finish in order to pay off the window, Ms. Moore had an accident. Rachel was repotting again—an endless task in the greenhouse—when Vivian came running into the greenhouse.

"Rachel," she cried, "come help me! Ms. Moore is hurt!" She looked strange, scared like Rachel had never seen her before. She ran back out, heading for the main house. Rachel dropped the pot she was working on and ran after her.

Ms. Moore was on the entryway floor near the foot of the stairs, her face twisted with pain and what looked to Rachel like embarrassment. Rachel wasn't sure, because she had never seen Ms. Moore look anything close to embarrassed before. Her steely hair was frazzled, the normally bulletproof bun she always wore threatening to come loose. Her dress (Ms. Moore never wore anything but dresses) was askew, revealing her stockings. The left stocking was frayed at the top, from much use and just as much laundering. She was trying to pull her dress hem down, but couldn't move without gasping in distress. Vivian settled by her head and held her shoulders. "She fell," she said to Rachel. Then, to Ms. Moore, "I called Dr. Beller and he's on his way. We shouldn't move you, he said, until he gets here."

Rachel grabbed some pillows from the sofa in the parlor and handed them to Vivian. "These will make her more comfortable." While Vivian put them under her head, Rachel pulled at Ms. Moore's dress, trying to get the skirt out from under her.

"Rachel, stop!" Vivian's face was bloodless, her hands shaking. "You're going to hurt her."

"Leave the child be," said Ms. Moore, in a voice wracked with effort. "I won't have Beller waltzing in here to see my delicates exposed in all their glory. I guess that old saying about wearing holey underwear has proved true." Then she made a sound low in her throat, a strange sound. The sound kept coming, burbling up and out, higher and wider. It seemed impossible, but Ms. Moore was laughing! Vivian and Rachel stared at each other and then both looked down at Ms. Moore.

"Um . . ." said Vivian, "yes, Ms. Moore, that does seem to be . . ." and then she burst into giggles. That made Rachel giggle too, even as she managed to get the dress smoothed down over Ms. Moore's legs.

"Enough of this frivolity, now," said Ms. Moore. Vivian

and Rachel immediately pasted on serious faces. "I will need to have access to a certain box, Ms. Quillen. It's in the desk in my study, a black box, with silver fastenings. The desk key is here." Ms. Moore always wore a chain around her neck on which hung several antique metal keys and an odd, old-looking ring made of some silver metal. She selected one of the keys and took it off, handing it to Vivian. "If you would be so kind as to take the box to my bedroom. Also, if you could see to my room, I believe the breakfast tray had not yet been cleared when this incident occurred."

Even when she was in excruciating pain, Ms. Moore was worried about someone seeing her room in an untidy state. Rachel couldn't decide if she admired Ms. Moore for this or thought she was silly.

"And you, Rachel," she said, when Vivian had gone to do her bidding. "If you would just . . . stay until Dr. Beller arrives, I would appreciate it." Ms. Moore's face had taken on a peculiar sheen, as though she had just finished a brisk set of aerobic exercise. Her breathing was ragged, and there were tears springing from the corners of her eyes. "So stupid! A simple slip on the stairs and look what becomes of me. I think I've managed to break my leg."

Ms. Moore's reserve had always been part of the backdrop of Rachel's childhood, a constant in her experience. Today, she had seen her both laugh and cry. It made Rachel wonder again what Ms. Moore was hiding behind her carefully arranged facade. What did she do in the evenings before she went upstairs to bed? Did she wish her life were different? What *did* she know about the Line, about Away? Rachel had been so busy—working in the greenhouse, learning about orchids—she hadn't had much time to devise a plan to discover Ms. Moore's secrets. Her one attempt to quiz Ms. Moore had failed miserably.

"Of course I'll stay, Ms. Moore," Rachel said. She took Ms. Moore's cold hand in hers.

Ms. Moore's leg *was* broken. Dr. Beller, an ancient man with a stooped back and only about two gray hairs left on his head, wanted her to go to the clinic in Bensen, where she could have proper medical care and rest. Ms. Moore, however, insisted that she would not leave The Property.

"I can rest as well here as in the clinic," she said. "Ms. Quillen will be here to see to my needs. I'm certain we shall manage."

Once Dr. Beller realized she wasn't going to change her mind, he agreed to set and cast her leg on The Property. He had what he needed to do it; Bensen was a long way if there was an emergency out in one of the rural areas, so his vehicle was well stocked with medical supplies. He had Rachel help him bring the supplies up the stairs to Ms. Moore's bedroom, where they had managed to move her after the doctor's initial examination on the floor downstairs. "I will have to anesthetize you in order to set it," he told Ms. Moore. "It would hurt quite a bit if you were conscious."

"In that case, Dr. Beller," Ms. Moore said, "I believe we should settle our accounts prior to the procedure." Dr. Beller started to object, saying there was no need to worry, but Ms.

Moore gestured toward the box Vivian had brought to her bedroom.

"Ms. Quillen, if you could bring that to me, please. And if you would be so kind as to return after the doctor and I have concluded our business, I would prefer it if you were present during the procedure. I will call you as soon as we are ready." Vivian set the box on the bed next to Ms. Moore and left the room. Ms. Moore took a different key from her chain and fit it into the lock on the box. "I suppose this is going to be expensive, Dr. Bell . . ." she began, and then stopped. She looked at the doorway, where Rachel still hovered. After a moment Rachel realized Ms. Moore was staring at her.

"Rachel!" Vivian materialized at the door, grabbed Rachel by the arm and pulled. "So sorry, Ms. Moore, I thought she was right behind me." Vivian tumbled Rachel out into the hall and down the stairs to the parlor. "Goodness, child, she told us to leave! What were you thinking?" Vivian's hair was escaping its combs, wavy auburn strands flying around her face.

"I'm sorry, Mom. I was . . . I wasn't thinking."

They heard Ms. Moore call "Ms. Quillen?" from above. Vivian took a deep breath and straightened her shoulders. "You," she said in her no-nonsense tone, "stay here, unless I call you. I shouldn't be long."

THAT EVENING, WHEN Ms. Moore was resting comfortably and Vivian and Rachel had retired to the guesthouse, it hit Vivian how much her daughter had grown up. Rachel had handled the accident with such great composure, not like the gangly girl Vivian was used to seeing. She was so composed, so caring. Vivian hadn't thought to get a pillow for Ms. Moore, hadn't thought of much at all beyond making sure she was alive and calling for the doctor. As soon as that was done, she had run, shaking, to get Rachel. The routine on The Property had made her feel almost safe, for a long time now. Seeing Ms. Moore hurt, not knowing if it meant the end of their sanctuary there, had unnerved her. But Rachel had been so calm; she saw what needed to be done, and she did it. It made Vivian feel proud. Proud and relieved— relieved that isolating Rachel here, sheltering her from so much, hadn't stopped her from growing into a good person.

It hadn't been easy since they lost Daniel. Not that it was exactly easy before that, always looking over their shoulders, always worried that the Ganivar Council would catch on to them. Wondering if a neighbor, or a vendor, or perhaps Julie, Rachel's babysitter, would suspect them and make a report. To look at Julie's sweet teenage face when she came to watch Rachel—she was the same age then that Rachel was now—and wonder if it concealed treachery. To know that Julie, an innocent child, had the power to have them all taken away, if she ever put two and two together. And most horrible of all, to know without a doubt that Julie would think she was doing the right thing, that she would feel *good* about turning them in to the Council.

When Daniel got the Call to Serve notice, Vivian knew from the look on his face as he read it that he would go. She wanted to run, try for Unifolle, try to start over. But Daniel said they would be caught. She remembered their arguments about it.

"We'd be safe in Unifolle, Daniel. The Council has no power there. They couldn't touch us."

"If we made it there, Viv. And how would we Cross?"

"We could go to Peter, ask him to let us use the key. You know he would." Vivian knew no such thing; the key wasn't much more than a rumor, a slip of the tongue one night during a dinner they'd had with their friends Peter and Jolie Hill. Their *only* friends really, and fellow collaborators. If it existed, the key would be protected the same way Daniel and Vivian would protect the maps they had been entrusted with; if Peter actually had it, he wouldn't admit it, even to friends.

"That's not something we should even be talking about." Daniel's eyes, his beautiful brown eyes, had met Vivian's, and she knew the look. He was serious. No matter what she said, he would not be moved. "Our other options are nonexistent. It's not just the Council we're dealing with; it's the whole government. You know as well as I do that they monitor the borders. And how would we even get permission to go on a trip? If they hadn't flagged our profiles before, you know they have now. Barry may not have made a report, but he certainly said something to someone. Why else would they have turned down my travel request?"

Daniel had filed a request for a day trip two weeks before, ostensibly to meet with Peter Hill about a project. Daniel often made travel requests as part of his job at Riser and Associates, an architectural firm in Ganivar. Peter, who was also an architect, lived in nearby Bensen, and they sometimes used the subterfuge of work to meet about collaboration matters. This latest request, however, had been denied by the Council, the first time that had happened. Daniel was certain that his boss, Barry Riser, was suspicious of him and had tipped off someone on the Council. They knew no formal report had been made, because if it had, they would have already been picked up. Barry had the kind of connections that would allow him to drop a comment at a cocktail party instead of making a formal report. That way, if his suspicions were unfounded, Daniel would never know Riser had doubted him, and if they were correct, Riser could avoid the negative publicity of having his business associated with a collaborator. Daniel and Vivian could be dealt with quietly, without the streamer coverage many exposures received. That was how it worked.

While the Council covertly investigated a suspected individual, travel requests and any other unusual activities—large cred transfers or withdrawals, vacation requests, or personal leave requests—would be prohibited. Daniel and Vivian had been waiting for something to happen ever since his travel request was denied. They got up every morning and tried to go through the motions of a normal life, wondering if today was the day they would be Identified. But they hadn't expected the Call to Serve.

A TEAR SLID down Vivian's cheek, and she wiped it away quickly before Rachel noticed. Oh, Rachel. She would have loved Daniel so. They would have had so many good times; they were so alike. But Rachel didn't even remember her own father. She would never know how brave he had been, how brave they had *both* been, because Vivian could never tell her. Her hands tightened into fists every time she thought of how much she and Rachel had lost when Daniel was sent over the Line.

She wasn't so brave now. She had a better idea of what she could lose. So she was hiding. Trying to keep Rachel safe. Every time she had to go to Bensen for supplies, she felt like a fugitive, wondering if Peter still lived there, wondering if he might spot her on the street. The Property had been her only chance to get Rachel out of Ganivar though. She was careful, and she tried to be sure that Rachel was careful. So far, they were safe.

Vivian couldn't help wondering how long that would last.

CHAPTER 6

Rachel hooked up the last of the hoses in the east section of the greenhouse and set the misting timer, wishing for at least the hundredth time that they could replace the worn-out set moldering on the storage shelf and have enough hoses for the whole place. She knew Ms. Moore must not have enough spare creds to do it, but it didn't stop her from wishing.

She was almost done for the day. Vivian had made the Bensen supply run without her today; there had been too much to do in the greenhouse for Rachel to go along as she usually did. As soon as she finished feeding the two-year-old phals, Rachel planned to go home and start dinner for herself and Vivian. Then she had to study for a history exam. Her mom had let her know that working in the greenhouse was not to interfere with her studying and so far it hadn't. She worked hard to make sure it didn't.

She hadn't made any headway at ferreting out Ms.

Moore's secret. Her leg still kept her out of the greenhouse most days, and on the few occasions she had made an appearance, she was all business. Whenever Rachel tried to start a conversation about something other than orchids, Ms. Moore simply gave her an odd look and started talking about fertilizers. Rachel didn't see how she could discover anything shocking about Ms. Moore if she couldn't even get her to talk about the weather.

Though she wasn't making progress with Ms. Moore, Rachel was learning a lot in the greenhouse. She was getting a feel for the orchids, and every time she found the beginning of a flower spike peeking out from beneath the leaves of a plant she felt happy. She was making things grow, helping things to blossom. It was the first time she had ever felt this excited about something. At least about something that was real.

Not all the results of her tending were so successful. She had lost her first batch of seedlings two days before. She had been sad ever since, and apprehensive too, of what Ms. Moore would think. Ms. Moore probably never lost seedlings. Rachel had disposed of the potting medium and sterilized the trays as soon as she knew for certain the seedlings would not survive, but she could still see the blackened mess in her head, little sprigs of new hope melted into slimy death. She couldn't figure out what had caused it. She had looked through the notes Ms. Moore had given her, and she thought she had followed every step correctly. But she must have done something wrong, or the baby orchids wouldn't have died.

Jonathan appeared at the greenhouse door as she fed the last of the phals.

"Ms. Moore wants you up at the main house," he said gravely. He examined the floor, carefully avoiding Rachel's eyes.

"Oh." Rachel was speechless for a moment. Ms. Moore never called her to the main house. She thought about it for a moment. "She knows about the seedlings, doesn't she?" Jonathan began to reply, but she put her hand on his arm before he could speak. "It's all right, Jonathan, I know you had to tell her. Don't feel bad. It's my fault." Rachel smiled what she hoped was a convincing smile. "Is she in the parlor?"

"Yes." Jonathan looked like he might say something more, but he reached for the plant food instead. "You'd better run along. She's expecting you. I'll close up."

Rachel thanked him and set off toward the main house, head down. She felt tears welling up as she trudged along and fought them back. She was going to miss working with the orchids. And her mom would be disappointed in her. Almost worse was the fact that *Ms. Moore* was disappointed in her. At least she had worked long enough to pay off the broken greenhouse pane.

Far too quickly, Rachel reached the front entrance to the house. It was grand; unlike anything she had seen in Bensen, where the houses were mostly small, one-story boxes. The apartment buildings were taller, but they were even plainer. The only bits of personality were the things one could glimpse through the different windows sometimes. Someone's houseplant, or the arm of a red chair.

Ms. Moore's house had a huge, covered front porch, held up by carved columns. There were two chairs arranged around a small table, though Rachel had never seen anyone sit in them. The front door was twice as tall as a man and wide enough to accommodate three people abreast easily. She pushed the black button to the right of the door and heard the chimes within, then the click of the intercom.

"Yes?" Ms. Moore's voice sounded hollow through the speaker next to the button.

Rachel cleared her throat, her mouth suddenly dry. "It's me, Ms. Moore. Rachel."

"Yes, Rachel," came the reply. "I've been expecting you. Come into the parlor, won't you?" The intercom clicked off.

Rachel opened the door and stepped into the large entryway. The tile floor gleamed, smoothed to an icy sheen from years of hand waxing. On a small table, a deep blue glass vase held a spray of creamy dendrobium blossoms. Rachel could smell the faint lemony scent of the special polish Ms. Moore had her mom use on the woodwork. Through the wide doorway that opened onto the parlor, she could see Ms. Moore seated in one of the matched set of chairs that flanked the fireplace. The chairs were large and looked soft, though Rachel had never sat in one of them. They reminded her of friendly sentries, keeping watch over the opening of a cave.

The first time Rachel had seen the fireplace, she had hardly believed it. It was a real one, not an image broadcast from a streamer screen. Sometimes in the winter Ms. Moore actually used it, burning old chair legs and other odd scraps of wood that Jonathan scavenged from various sources. Rachel was pretty sure Ms. Moore was breaking some conservation law when she did that. She wondered why Ms. Moore would do it, even though the risk of being caught way out here was slim. When she asked her mom, Vivian had shrugged and said that Ms. Moore probably liked the way it looked.

"But she could have the same thing if she installed an extra streamer and set it to one of the ambiance broadcasts. They aren't that expensive. And she could even choose different stuff, if she got tired of the Fire broadcast. She could choose Mountain Vistas, or the Living Seas. Why doesn't she just do that?" Rachel thought the fireplace was strange; when there was no fire burning, which was almost always, it was just a big empty box. Rachel thought it was ugly.

"But a streamer doesn't get hot, Rachel. You can't feel it. You can't smell the wood smoke. It's not . . . real." Vivian smiled and shook her head. "I know it seems weird. But she must remember having real fires from when she was a child. It's a comfort thing, like me wearing Dad's old socks, or you still wanting a bedtime story once in a while."

Rachel didn't think Ms. Moore seemed like the type to indulge in comfort things.

"Come in, child." Ms. Moore looked much more like

herself; better than she had looked since the accident. Her color was back, and her face gave away nothing of what she might be thinking. She motioned toward the sofa facing her. "Sit down. I want to talk with you."

Rachel perched on the sofa, a much more formal piece of furniture than the sentry chairs, not designed for snuggling or naps like the couch in the guesthouse. The fabric was a scratchy tweed, and the seat felt as hard as the floor. For a long moment neither of them said anything. Rachel swallowed, and cast her eyes around the room as if there might be a friendlier version of Ms. Moore hiding in a corner somewhere. Her gaze fell on the mantel; there, next to a tiny glass box, was the digim that her mother had mentioned. Rachel had not seen it many times; at the employee dinners they generally went straight to the dining room on the opposite side of the entryway. The day of Ms. Moore's accident, Rachel hadn't had time to look at it closely.

The digim was in a silver frame. It was an old-fashioned, static 3-D digim, no animation or audio, so it revealed nothing of the subject besides his appearance. The man in it was young, about how old her father looked in the digims at home in the portfolio. He had dark hair that was long enough to curl around his face. He was smiling, a smile that looked like the beginning of a soft laugh. His eyes were the bluest eyes Rachel had ever seen on a human being. Vivian had blue eyes, but they were a soft blue, like the sky in the morning. This man's eyes were blue like the vase in the entry, lapis blue. Rachel knew he wasn't Ms. Moore's husband, because Ms. Moore said she had never been married when Vivian asked. Who could he be?

"Rachel, would you mind?" Ms. Moore's voice broke the silence and Rachel's contemplation of the mystery digim. "I had your mother fix us some kalitea before she left for Bensen, but I'm afraid my leg is being troublesome today."

Rachel noticed the cups and saucers on the table between them for the first time. "Oh, yes, Ms. Moore. I can do that." Rachel stood to pour kalitea for each of them, holding her breath as she handled the delicate teapot. She sat back down on the edge of the hard sofa cushion, holding her cup while it cooled. "Thank you, Ms. Moore. For the kalitea, I mean."

"You are very welcome, Rachel." Ms. Moore took a sip from her cup. "I wanted to ask you—"

"I understand, Ms. Moore," Rachel blurted. She couldn't keep it in any longer. "I know that I messed up. I still don't know what happened, I've thought and thought, and I sterilized everything like the notes said, and I watered just so much, not too much, but they still died. I am so sorry. And I understand why you wouldn't want me working anymore. I have paid off the window though, so at least there's that, and I truly am so sorry."

Ms. Moore sat for a moment, saying nothing. Her eyes had widened ever so slightly. She set her cup and saucer down on the table next to her chair and furrowed her brow. "Rachel," she said, "are you talking about the tray of seedlings Jonathan told me about?"

"Yes." Rachel felt horrible. Was there something else she had done wrong, that she didn't even know about?

"Well, that is one of the reasons I wanted to talk with you today. But only because Jonathan mentioned that you seem sad. He thought the seedlings might have something to do with it."

Rachel blinked. "I am sad." She felt tears flooding her eyes again and blinked harder. "I *killed* them."

Ms. Moore looked alarmed at the possibility of some sort of emotional outburst. She straightened her back, plucked at her skirt for a moment, removing an invisible speck of lint. Rachel snuffled with increasing force. Ms. Moore abandoned her skirt after the third repressed snuffle from Rachel, produced a linen handkerchief and held it out. Then she held up one hand in the universal signal for stop. This brought Rachel's tears to an abrupt halt, as though even they were intimidated.

"Rachel." Ms. Moore waved away the handkerchief, which Rachel, after using it to blow her nose, was trying to return. "Losing seedlings is a part of the work. You did your best and that is all that can be expected. Sometimes there is no reason, at least that you can see, for losing them. You can do everything right and they will still die." She smiled. "Why, if I counted the trays of seedlings I've lost in my day, trays I had high hopes for, in fact, that might have become very special crosses. You just have to keep trying."

Rachel thought about the feeling she got when that tray of seedlings took hold, when their waxy green leaves began to form into tiny replicas of what the adult plants would look like. It felt like she was creating something important, something that went out into the world and made a little difference. The shipments of orchids that Jonathan took to town were *all* once just seedlings; tiny green sprigs of possibility. She wanted to see her own seedlings grow into beautiful blooms too.

She liked to imagine the journey the orchids took, from the greenhouse to the vendors' stalls, where they were put into buckets of water, waiting for someone to notice them. She liked to think about who might pass by and see the ideal red or the impossible blue of a bloom, and feel themselves drawn into it. She could picture a woman buying a single, perfect orchid and carrying it home, to an apartment somewhere. She could see the woman getting a vase down from a cupboard, filling it with water and placing the orchid in it just so, tilting it a bit this way or that, setting it in the middle of a table, standing back to admire it. Smiling.

Ms. Moore's voice interrupted Rachel's daydream. "Unless, of course, you don't *want* to keep trying. It may seem like too much work to you." Ms. Moore took a dainty sip of her kalitea, her eyes lowered to the rim of her cup.

Rachel hadn't really known how much it mattered to her until today, when it seemed as though she wouldn't be able to do it anymore. "I do want to keep trying, Ms. Moore," she said. "I love the greenhouse. I just assumed you wouldn't want me to work there anymore . . ." Rachel struggled to keep tears from falling onto her cheeks.

Ms. Moore spoke quickly, as if she hoped her words could forestall another disturbing display of emotion.

"I asked you here today because I wanted to see if you *would* be interested in learning more about growing orchids, Rachel. I may need more help in the greenhouse from now on. You seem to have the aptitude, and you also seem to enjoy the work. Those are both important things. But there is so much more to it than what you know now. It would take serious study if you were to advance enough to be of real assistance.

"I have, of course, discussed it with your mother already, and she feels that as long as your schoolwork doesn't suffer, the decision is up to you." Ms. Moore paused for a moment. "Would you like more kalitea, Rachel? I would love a bit more, if you don't mind."

While Rachel poured, Ms. Moore continued. "As I said, in order to help me, you would need to learn more. That would require more studying on your part. Which would mean that you would earn more, as well. I can't pay you much more than I do now, but it would help, perhaps, with college. Your mother tells me you plan to attend somewhere once your primary studies are completed." Ms. Moore picked up the teacup Rachel had filled and sipped.

Rachel was surprised that Ms. Moore knew about her college plans. Her mother kept most of their personal business to herself.

"I *am* planning to go to college," Rachel said. "My mom thinks it's important that I learn all I can about how the world really is, but we still need to save more for tuition." Rachel added some sugar to her tea. "If I could help Mom with that, it would be great."

"How the world really is?" Ms. Moore's eyebrows rose. "Your mother thinks you might learn that at a college?"

"Not just any college." Rachel was surprised at how loud her voice sounded and she could feel her face getting hot. Ms. Moore had no right to criticize what her mother thought. "She wants me to go to the right kind of college, the kind where they teach the truth about things, not just what they're supposed to tell you." Rachel wanted to say more, but she was afraid she had already said too much.

Ms. Moore just smiled. "I'm sure that your mother is right, Rachel," she said. "Perhaps I've just stopped believing that ordinary people are *ever* told the truth about things." Ms. Moore stopped speaking then, and for what seemed like a long while she gazed somewhere above Rachel's head. Rachel was puzzling over what she had said, when Ms. Moore finally stirred, and smiled once again. "I want you to think about our conversation and let me know in a few days. In the meantime you should take some time off from the greenhouse, a little vacation. Jonathan can keep up with the daily maintenance for a short while. If you do take the job you'll be quite busy with working and studying. A rest first would be good."

"I don't even have to think about it, Ms. Moore," Rachel said. "I know I would like to learn more. I don't need a rest. I could come in tomorrow morning as usual." Rachel was relieved that Ms. Moore hadn't thought better of her offer. "I didn't mean to be rude about colleges, Ms. Moore."

"Rachel," said Ms. Moore, looking at her carefully. "It is never rude to respectfully state one's opinion. We simply have different thoughts on the subject." Ms. Moore set her teacup down on the table between them, her movement signaling the end of the meeting as clearly as a judge's gavel. "Thank you for joining me today. I am glad you want to learn more about the orchids, but I still want you to take a few days for yourself. A bit of free time never hurt anyone. You can start back on Monday."

Rachel hesitated for a moment, but she knew now was as good a time as any to try to find out more about Ms. Moore's mysterious past. "Ms. Moore," she said, keeping her eyes on her teacup, "I was wondering . . ." Rachel had to think about how to go on. "I was wondering whether you ever think of moving to Bensen, or Ganivar, or somewhere . . . not so close to the Line." Rachel saw Ms. Moore stiffen, and she finished her question in a rush. "Lots of people seem scared of it."

Ms. Moore was watching her closely.

"Why," said Ms. Moore, "would I be afraid of a simple barrier that some ignorant military committee ordered built?" Her voice was hard. Rachel was almost afraid to speak, but she managed to squeak out her next question.

"Because of . . . Away? Because of the things people say about—"

Ms. Moore cut Rachel off, her tone as sharp as a china

shard. "You know nothing of Away. And it's best not to speak of things you don't know about. Perhaps once you attend the *right* college you'll learn something about that." She rose slowly from her seat. "I need to rest a bit now," she said. "I will see you in the greenhouse on Monday."

Their meeting was clearly over.

Rachel walked down the path to home. She thought about how angry Ms. Moore had been at her questions. There was something behind it, something Ms. Moore didn't want anyone to know. She was pretty sure that it was something about Away. The skin prickled on her neck, though the day was mild. The idea that Ms. Moore knew something about that frightening, shadowy place didn't really scare her. The idea that whatever she knew caused her voice to shake the way it had in the parlor—*that* scared Rachel plenty.

CHAPTER 7

Rachel!" Vivian inhaled deeply as she kicked off her shoes. She was back from Bensen and Ms. Moore's supplies were all put away, so she was done for the day. "Did you make dinner again?"

"Yes. I thought you would probably be tired since you had to lug all the supplies around by yourself today. I'm sorry I couldn't go help."

"You had enough to do at the greenhouse today." Vivian inhaled again. "Whatever that is, it smells delicious."

"It's that rice dish you made, the one with the asparagus, remember?" Rachel pulled out a chair at the table for Vivian and made an exaggerated, sweeping gesture. "Have a seat, milady."

"Oh, this is so nice." Vivian sank into the chair. "Especially nice, because I have to go back to Bensen *again* tomorrow. Most of the vendors had nothing today. Another transit breakdown. So none of their shipments were delivered. It seems like every other week one of the transit vehicles breaks down or the refrigeration malfunctions and everything is ruined. So much for government efficiency."

"I can go with you and help tomorrow. Ms. Moore gave me vacation until Monday." Rachel put the bowl of rice casserole on the table and sat down. "She had me over for a *meeting* today."

"I thought she might." Vivian tried to look innocent, but when she saw Rachel's face, she laughed.

Rachel swatted at her with her napkin. "You could have warned me. I thought I was going to get fired!"

"Fired? Why would she fire you? You're doing very well at the greenhouse."

"I don't know." Rachel shrugged. "You know how she is—hard to tell what might make her mad."

"Did you take the job?"

"Yes. It's okay, right? I mean, Ms. Moore said she talked to you about it."

"It's fine. And I think you deserve a vacation." Vivian considered for a moment. "I think you can even have a vacation from . . . schoolwork!"

Rachel just stared. She *never* got vacations from schoolwork. "Mom!"

"Just be sure that on Monday evening you're back at it right after you finish at the greenhouse. When you get to college, I don't want you to be behind the others. Understood?" Vivian spoke in a stern voice, which dissolved into a giggle when Rachel saluted and said, "Understood, yes, ma'am!" in her best military voice.

"I'll still go with you tomorrow though, okay?"

"Sure, honey. I'll be leaving tomorrow afternoon. You can take the morning for whatever you want. Just be sure you stay out of trouble."

THE NEXT MORNING, after she tidied up the breakfast dishes, Rachel decided to take a book and a picnic and spend some time outside. The book was one she had checked out from the Bensen library during the last trip she made with her mother. A real book, about orchids. She would have to return it soon and she hadn't had much time to read it. She packed some cheese, a bottle of water, and an apple, and set out.

The Property covered ten acres, and Rachel had not explored it all. Vivian had always told Rachel that she must not venture outside the area Jonathan maintained around the buildings. That included the main house, the garage, the greenhouse, and the guesthouse, and it was over three acres in all. Plenty of room for all kinds of imaginary kingdoms and games. Meadows surrounded most of the lawn, gradually giving way to forest. One of Rachel's favorite places was the west meadow, where a stream flowed into a small pool. She decided to go there.

There were late summer flowers springing up along the stream's banks, and Rachel could hear a frog croaking somewhere in the reeds as she approached. It fell silent as she settled into the nook of a tree stump near the tiny pool. Her back fit into the stump's curve perfectly. From this seat she had dreamed up countless diversions for herself when she was younger.

She looked around at the meadow surrounding her, taking in the sunlit grasses swaying in the light breeze and breathing in the fresh, cool air. Then she opened her book and began to read about a different method of germinating orchids, one that Ms. Moore didn't use. Rachel was thinking of trying it. Soon the frog resumed its singing, and some sparrows that had flown away to a nearby tree at her arrival ventured back to the pool to drink.

Rachel was happily lost in her book for some time. Once, a dragonfly buzzed by her, investigating her presence. The iridescent flash of its wings caught her attention for a moment, but she soon went back to her reading. The germination method the author described seemed fairly simple, and it promised less chance of rot. Rachel wasn't sure she could get permission to try it, but she thought Ms. Moore might let her if she showed her the percentage of healthy plants the book's author claimed it yielded compared to the method they used now.

"Caw-caaaaw!" Rachel jerked in surprise and looked up from her book. A huge black crow was stalking along the edge of the pool, screeching at something. He looked indignant, as though he was personally affronted at whatever he saw there, which made Rachel laugh. At the sound of her giggle, the crow darted his head toward her, one glittering eye glaring for a moment, then dismissed her and turned back to the pool. "Caw-ca-aaaw!!" he screamed. He hopped back and forth, toward the edge of the pool and away, agitated.

"What is it, buddy?" Rachel put her book down and sat up straight, craning to see over the reeds that fringed her view. The crow screamed again, skipping sideways away from her. Rachel stood and the crow turned to face her. "I'm not going to hurt you, buddy," Rachel said, starting toward him. With a muffled clap of his wings, the crow leaped into the air, swooping upward and screeching the whole way. "Sorry," Rachel muttered, and walked closer to the pool to see what he had been so excited about.

At first she saw nothing unusual, just the water flowing around in lazy swirls, making its way to the pool's outlet, where it would bounce and bubble along the rock stream-bed and off to oblivion. Then Rachel caught a glimmer on the water's surface. The sun reflecting off the ripples? No, it was something silver, floating in lazy spirals on the water, trapped in an eddy. She leaned out over the pool, trying to see what it was, but couldn't tell. She broke a long reed off and poked at the object until she had it by an edge. Care-fully, she maneuvered it toward her. She almost lost it to the current when she tried to get it clear of the eddy, but she was able to catch it again and bring it close enough to grab. With her free hand, she plucked it from the water.

It was a thin, flat rectangle of silver-colored plastic, smaller than a playing card. It looked much like the corder Rachel's mother kept in a box of odds and ends from her college days, except Vivian's was black and less battered around the edges. This one had the same three buttons on the front, one to activate the audio recording mechanism, one to rewind and fast-forward, one for playback, though they were of a clumsier, older-looking design than the buttons on her mom's. Vivian's still had part of a lecture on Renaissance artists on it from a long-ago class. Rachel had played with it when she was little, fast-forwarding endlessly to turn the instructor's sonorous voice into skittering chipmunk chirps.

She wiped the corder on her pants to remove as much water as possible. Her mom's corder used the energy generated from the rewind and fast-forward functions to continually recharge its tiny batteries. This one was older than her mom's, but Rachel thought it might work the same way. She pushed the playback button. At first there was nothing, but after a moment the tiny speaker on the back emitted some scratchy sounds. A few seconds more and Rachel heard a voice. It was a male voice, but nothing like that of the long-ago college instructor. This voice sounded friendlier and sad. The words were hard to understand, and parts of the recording were nothing but static. Rachel hit the rewind button and played it again.

"Hello," the voice said, followed by some static. Then, "indigo . . . forgive . . . we are desperate . . . help." More static, then, ". . . if you live . . . danger . . . would not ask if . . . choice. Our . . . die if we cannot get medicine . . . he will wait near the edge . . . green house each day at sunset . . . this message . . . will explain. Please help us."

Rachel stared at the corder. She rewound it again and played the message, straining to hear more words through the static. When she realized she wouldn't be able to, she walked back to her book near the stump and sat down to think. A message. But from whom, and why? Rachel shook the corder hard to get more water out. She set it on a rock in the sun and ate some of her picnic food while she waited for the corder to dry out a bit more. Soon she would have to go back home, because she had promised to go to Bensen with her mother that afternoon.

After a while she tried the corder again, but the message was no more understandable than before. The words that struck her most were "wait near the edge," "green house," and "please help us." The green house had to mean *their* greenhouse, the greenhouse on The Property. Someone wanted to meet near the greenhouse. They needed help. And that thing about "indigo"; what was that? The person said it twice, but she couldn't figure out what it meant. The corder looked pretty old and beat-up, but the date stamp on the message was only two weeks ago.

She gathered her book and picnic things and slipped the corder into her pocket. She would make it back just in time to meet Vivian if she hurried. The message would have to wait. Who could the person be? Whom did he want to meet? Rachel wondered if she should show Vivian, but she didn't think she would. It was a mystery, a sort of adventure, and she wanted to keep it to herself for a while longer. Her mom thought everything was dangerous. If she told Vivian about the corder, Rachel knew that she would never see it again.

She studied the pool for a moment, watching the water from the stream spill into it. Where did the stream come from? She imagined the tiny corder tumbling along on its way to the pool. On its way to her. Then she turned and walked quickly toward home.

CHAPTER 8

VIVIAN AND RACHEL took the greenhouse utility vehicle to Bensen when they went for supplies. A fine, almost luxurious passenger vehicle was kept charged in the garage next to the main house, but it was covered in a thick layer of dust. Ms. Moore had used it when she still went to town. She had not been to town even once since Vivian and Rachel had come to The Property. So the beautiful vehicle slumbered, a softly glowing red light on the charging meter the only indication it still had any life in it. The utility vehicle was dirty and dinged, but the seats were comfortable. It had ferried Rachel and her mother back and forth to Bensen many times, bouncing over the rough roads dependably.

The long drive to Bensen was always fun for Rachel. Her mother was usually in a good mood, feeling free and laughing. Today was no different. Vivian asked how Rachel's first day off had been, and Rachel said it was fine. She told her mother about reading by the stream and having a picnic, but she didn't mention the corder. Vivian had her read the list of supplies out loud, so she could make sure there was nothing missing that they might need during the next week. By the time they pulled into Bensen, they had added two items; some honey for Ms. Moore's breakfast muffins and some fresh fish for their own dinner. Fresh fish was pricey, and they rarely indulged.

"What's the occasion?" Rachel asked, wondering at the extravagance.

"We'll have a little celebration of your vacation," said Vivian. Her mother's mood turned serious for a moment. "You should enjoy this time, Rachel. You're smart and safe and free and . . ." Then she giggled and spoke in a high, eighty-year-old-lady-imparting-words-of-wisdom voice. "You're only young once, as they say, my dear. Live life to the fullest and thank the stars you have your health. Now, let's get shopping!"

Rachel rolled her eyes, but she laughed.

Bensen's shopping district was always busy, at least whenever Rachel saw it, with lots of different vendors. According to Vivian, it was possible to find almost everything you could find in larger cities like Ganivar if you knew where to look. Rachel didn't remember Ganivar at all; she couldn't imagine living in a town even as big as Bensen. It was a little overwhelming. She did like to visit though, to watch how the people behaved.

There were so *many* people, some rushing, looking like they were late for appointments, some strolling along as though they had all the time in the world. Two men stand-ing outside a cred center were disagreeing about something in low, heated voices. A Labor Pool crew was repairing the water pipes in the street. They all wore gray jumpsuits with *LP* emblazoned on them in big black letters. Two of the men from the crew were down in a hole, handing tools up to a boy who looked younger than Rachel. On the corner in front of the fish vendor's, a woman in a red coat leaned down to wipe the strawberry ice cream off her child's face and laughed when the little girl promptly smeared more on.

It didn't take long for Vivian and Rachel to collect the items they needed. Their last stop was the fish store. Inside, a man argued with the vendor about the price of a salmon. The vendor argued back for a while about the rate of his taxes. Finally, he just folded his arms and waited to see if the man wanted the fish or not.

Rachel and her mother were next in line.

"Well, Rachel, what do you feel like having?"

Rachel surveyed the selection. "The trout looks good," she said finally, "if that's okay with you too?"

"Trout it is, then." Vivian smiled at the vendor and pointed to one of the fish in the display. "That one looks nice," she said, handing over her cred card.

"That is a fine choice, ma'am." The vendor weighed the fish and wrapped it. After swiping her card, he handed it back to Vivian along with the fish.

"Thanks," Vivian said, and she followed Rachel toward the exit.

"That trout is going to be delicious, Mom." Rachel grinned at Vivian over her shoulder, then turned to open the door. "Can we fix it with that salad, like we did last time?" She stopped suddenly, halfway through the door. Vivian, unaware that Rachel had stopped moving, ran right into her, and they both stumbled out onto the sidewalk.

"Rachel, you almost made me drop the . . ." Vivian stopped.

Rachel stared across the street, where a small crowd had gathered. The woman Rachel had seen earlier, the one in the red coat, was in the center of the crowd. Her arms were out-stretched to her child, but she was roughly restrained by an Enforcement Officer. Two feet away from her, her little girl was screaming, her livid face slick with tears. She was strug-gling to reach her mother, but another EO had hooked his baton into the collar of her jacket. He was laughing because the little girl didn't understand why she couldn't make any forward progress. The woman jerked her arm, trying to shake the EO's hold on her and get to her daughter. The EO slapped her hard across the face. The little girl's screams grew louder.

"Mom!" Rachel started toward the scene, alarmed at how rough the officers were being.

"No, Rachel." Vivian's voice was low, but as hard as the grip she had on her daughter's wrist. Rachel looked back, surprised, and the expression on her mother's face fright-ened her. Vivian pulled Rachel back into the shop and let the door swing closed. She stood for moment, still holding Rachel's wrist. She was shaking.

"Mom?" Rachel was torn between her urge to go help the woman outside and her concern over her mother.

"Rachel, follow me back to the counter and be quiet." Vivian whispered the instructions, smiling incongruously at Rachel the whole time. "Act as though there is nothing wrong at all."

"But, Mom ..." Rachel started to protest, but her mother tightened her grip and turned to go.

"Just do what I say," Vivian hissed, still smiling grimly. She walked back toward the vendor with Rachel in tow.

"Forget something, folks?" The fish vendor had finished with his other customer. He put his hands on his hips and surveyed the cases. "The salmon is pretty good, and the halibut is on sale right now if you like white fish."

"That's what we were thinking," Vivian said, her voice a note too bright. "Some of that halibut would be perfect." She stared at the vendor, keeping her smile fixed in place.

The vendor looked past her though, out the window to the street. "Look at that," he said, walking out from behind the counter. "Looks like some trouble out there." He moved closer to the window.

"Oh?" Vivian half turned. "I hadn't noticed."

"Yeah, looks like government men ... well, I think that's an Identification!" The vendor opened the door for a better look. "We haven't seen one of those in Bensen in years."

The other customer, an old man with gray hair, shuffled toward the door as well. "Been at least ten years since the last one if I recall," he said. "I think I'll have a closer look."

"Ma'am, if you don't mind waiting for a minute, I have to see this." The vendor smiled and shrugged sheepishly at Vivian. "It's the most excitement there's been around here for a long time. I'll come right back." He left without waiting to hear Vivian's reply.

Once the shop was empty, Vivian's smile disappeared. "Rachel, get behind me and stay close. I'm going to wait until nobody is looking this way, and then we are going to get out of here as fast as we can." She held the door open a few inches, peeking out.

"Mom, what are you talking about?" Now that Rachel knew what was happening to the woman across the street, she understood why Vivian didn't want to interfere. Her mom had always instructed her to stay far away from any government officers. And though she had never seen anything like it in Bensen, Rachel knew things like this happened; streamer coverage of Identifications was common. News announcers always described the incidents as "another example of your government at work protecting the public safety" and usually cited a long list of crimes committed by the person being Identified. None of the coverage showed such violent treatment though; Identifications were always quiet and orderly, if you believed the streamer coverage.

Rachel didn't understand why they had to *sneak* away. Everybody else was standing around staring. Even if Vivian wanted to avoid trouble, the woman in the red coat was the one in trouble, not them.

"Rachel"—her mother didn't even turn around—"when

we get back on the road, I have some things to tell you. Now stay close, we're going."

They slunk out the door, Rachel staying as close to her mother as she could. Once they were on the street, Vivian put her arm around Rachel and turned her toward the vendor's display window. She watched the crowd in the window's reflection, waiting for the right moment to move. When it seemed as though everyone's attention was fully on the Identification, Vivian hurried Rachel down the street.

One person in the crowd wasn't watching the Identification anymore. He had stopped paying attention to that as soon as he had noticed Vivian across the street. Her odd behavior interested him, and he followed her progress until she and Rachel disappeared around the corner. When he could no longer see them, he pushed his hat back off his forehead in a thoughtful way, then turned and walked in the opposite direction.

CHAPTER 9

Vivian pulled off onto a side road and found a place hidden by a grove of trees where they could park unobserved. She took a deep breath and gripped the steering wheel hard to stop her hands from shaking. When she spoke, her words were ragged and rushed.

"Rachel, I need you to understand how dangerous it is to attract attention of *any* kind when we're in Bensen. We cannot take chances like the one you almost took back there. Those EOs would have been just as happy to haul you away with . . . with that woman. They don't need a reason; they can do whatever they want. In this society—"

"I know all that from your school assignments, Mom." Rachel stared at Vivian. She felt like she was looking at an impostor. Could this possibly be the same person who constantly talked about the injustices the government imposed on people? This person, who had just scuttled out of town like a sheep when she saw it in action? Rachel couldn't quite believe that they had *run away*, like *cowards*, from the scene in Bensen. She didn't think of herself as a coward. She had never thought of Vivian as one before either.

Vivian shook her head. "Rachel, you only know what the government wants you to know."

"I know what *you* teach me, Mom. You're the one who makes the assignments."

"And where do you think I get the reading materials I assign?" Vivian said. "I've got nothing but official texts to work with. The only thing you've read that hasn't been a sanitized government version of the facts is the Bill of Rights, Rachel. The *old* one. And the official—"

"The official story isn't necessarily the true story." Rachel rolled her eyes. "I know. You've made me write so many essays about how the government is corrupt that I could probably get arrested just for that. I know that the government lies. I *know*." Rachel shrugged. "But guess what, Mom? It doesn't seem like it matters that I know that. *Justice*. You always talk about it, but we just watched EOs practically beat a woman and we skulked away. How's that for justice?" Rachel turned her head and looked out the window at the trees.

Vivian sighed, exasperated. "Do you even know how EOs came to be, Rachel?" Her daughter didn't look at her. "Well, do you?"

"The Michaels execution." Rachel finally looked back at Vivian. She spoke mechanically, reciting the lesson by rote. "After the execution, the police couldn't control the protesters, so the government formed the Enforcement Department. The EOs were given special training and more power than the police. They had to have more power so they could effectively restore order."

"Well, that's the official version," said Vivian. She looked down at her hands, still gripping the steering wheel. "Do you know," she said, without raising her eyes, "why Michaels was executed, Rachel? Why so many people protested that they had to form a special force to control them?"

"He committed treason." Rachel looked at her mother, frowning, remembering the details of the history assignment. "He was a news writer, made accusations about government officials in his column, and wouldn't reveal his sources. He was jailed for refusing to name them. The government claimed the accusations he made were a threat to national security. But some people thought the death penalty wasn't merited. We studied that—the fact that the government was killing a man for speaking out against them. And about how so many of the people who protested when they executed Michaels were Identified and locked up. So?" Rachel leaned forward to peer at her mother's face. Vivian was still staring at her hands.

"Mom?" Rachel waited a moment. "Mom?"

Vivian finally met Rachel's gaze. "Michaels was one of the first collaborators. Many of those people who protested were too. They were the beginning. And now the collaborators have members everywhere."

Vivian reached for Rachel's hand, held it in her own, stroking it. "Your father," she whispered, "was a member. So was I."

Rachel stared at her mother's face. "You were . . ." She stuttered to silence. She knew what collaborators were, sort of. People who fought the wrongs of the government, people who led shadowy, hidden lives, doing illegal things in the name of freedom. Vivian's homeschool lessons had always emphasized that the government reports calling collaborators "criminals" and "threats to society" were nothing more than political dogma. She called the collaborators "revolutionaries."

"We were collaborators." Vivian held her hand tighter. "Your father didn't go fight in that war because he believed in the cause. He went because he was sent. The government was on to us, and they sent your father to serve in that war as a punishment. It was an easy way to get rid of him. You and I moved to The Property because we had to, after he was gone."

"I don't understand, Mom." Rachel was bewildered. "You told me Dad was a successful architect. You said we had a good life. Why would the two of you have been collaborators?"

"I'm going to explain it, Rachel. So you *will* understand." Vivian turned in her seat so she was facing Rachel. She said nothing for a few moments, gathering her thoughts.

Rachel watched different expressions flicker across Vivian's face, but she was unfamiliar with every one of them. She felt as though she had just stepped off a curb where none was expected; that odd, fleeting sense of weightlessness when one's foot encounters a void instead of solid ground.

Finally, Vivian spoke.

"We did have a good life. It made us perfect recruits for the collaboration. In college we had spotless backgrounds, the prospect of good jobs, and we could move through society without rousing suspicion. But we also had reasons to hate that society, Rachel. Reasons like your father's childhood friend Alex. Your father told me so many stories about him. He said Alex was bright and promising, full of hope. He painted watercolors, and he wrote poetry—wonderful poetry, according to Daniel."

Rachel shook her head. "What does Dad's childhood friend have to do with being collaborators?"

"It's what happened to him, Rachel. Alex was a factory worker's son. He was denied the chance to explore his talents, to go to college like Daniel, to ever earn more than enough to survive, simply because his father didn't have the money to secure an admission. He took the general population exams and easily qualified, but there were more secured admissions than openings. You'll be taking those exams soon enough, Rachel. And no matter how well you do on them, you wouldn't get into any college at all if I didn't have certain . . . savings . . . set aside."

"You mean the tuition creds?"

"No." Vivian shook her head. "That will only cover *tuition*. People need a lot more than that to get into college. I have some extra savings I brought with us when we came here. Your father and I . . . we had some black-market gold. I plan to use it to get you a secured admission. Otherwise, you would be in exactly the same position your dad's friend Alex was."

Vivian was silent for so long that Rachel wondered if she was going to continue. When she did, her voice was much softer.

"It used to be that if you were smart and hardworking, you could go to college no matter who you were, Rachel. At least you had a chance. But things like secured admissions to college became routine a long time ago, before your father and I were even born. It became normal to have to buy your way into college. If you don't have the creds or the connections, your choices in life are limited. Most people just accept their lot, because there really isn't anything they can do about it.

"But your father's friend Alex was crushed. He couldn't accept what happened to him; he wanted more. He was young and a dreamer, and he thought he would die if he couldn't live his dreams. Who knows, perhaps he would have. Perhaps he would have wasted away in the factory, if he was lucky enough to get a position there, dreams drying up one by one. Perhaps his mind would have slowly filled with the deadly gray of assembly work, year after year." A tear escaped the corner of Vivian's eye. She hastily wiped it away.

"Alex didn't wait to see what would happen. When Daniel left for college, Alex hung himself. His father found him when he returned from a shift at the factory—a limp, lifeless body in place of his laughing, handsome son.

"Daniel never forgot it, nor did he forgive himself. His admission to college had nothing to do with Alex being denied, at least not directly. Daniel's admission had been secured by his father, your grandfather, when he was still a toddler. But he always blamed himself anyway. He said he was a part of the system. He said he might as well have killed Alex himself."

By the time Vivian finished recounting Alex's story, Rachel was weeping. Not just for Alex, though his story broke her heart. She was weeping for her father. She would never hear his stories or be able to talk to him about things. He would have known *exactly* what to do about the corder. He would have *never* slunk away from the Identification. Rachel loved Vivian. But at that moment she missed having a dad more than she ever had before.

"You okay?" Vivian handed Rachel a tissue.

Rachel nodded. "I'm okay. I guess I can't understand why people would let things like that happen." Rachel didn't want to tell her mom the real reasons she was crying.

"Oh, Rachel. Look at what they let happen now. So many people believe the propaganda the government distributes. You know how it is—you see the streamer coverage on the issues. It's the party line all the way. 'The Identification System is necessary for the safety of the people; all prisoners are justly incarcerated. Random taxes and all of the other government regulations are fair.' The costly licenses for marriage, restrictions on childbearing slanted in favor of those lucky enough to be rich or connected, Labor Pool sentences for those who can't prove Gainful Employment status. All of those things are accepted as requisite components of a healthy, working social system." Vivian smiled at Rachel. "At least by most people."

"But not Dad?" Rachel was still absorbing the thought that her own father—and her *mother*—were once collaborators. Vivian had always taught her to view the government with suspicion, but Rachel couldn't imagine her taking the kind of chances that collaborators must.

"Not your dad." Vivian swiped at her cheeks, wiping away a fresh round of tears. "Your dad knew better, Rachel, because of Alex. And he was brave. Most people are too afraid to protest, so they simply go along." She nodded to herself, remembering things, things that Rachel couldn't guess at.

"Your father and I couldn't just go along. We had to try to change things. In college we learned about the collaborators. There was a secret meeting, and we went." Vivian shook her head. "We trained. We studied. When it was time, we moved to Ganivar, set up house, played the happy, successful young couple. And collaborated.

"You should have seen how it was in Ganivar, Rachel. People were so afraid—their fear turned them into monsters. If a friend or colleague was Identified during lunch and hauled away, well, the thing to do was simply order dessert and change the subject. People looked the other way when their neighbor disappeared into the back of an Enforcement vehicle. They didn't want to know where that ride ended.

"We tried to be careful. But we weren't careful enough. Someone reported Daniel to the Ganivar Council. He was sent to war soon after."

She looked into Rachel's eyes, her gaze intense. "That's

why I couldn't let you interfere with the Identification today. That's why we've spent our lives hidden away on The Property. What if those EOs had scanned your genid, Rachel? You would have come up as Daniel Quillen's daughter. There's a big red flag next to your name just because he was your father. There was never any proof I was a collaborator, but they might think I would be happy to name names if they had my daughter to dangle in front of me as bait." Vivian took Rachel's hand. "I can't let anything happen to you, Rachel. You're all I have left."

Rachel was silent for a long while. "Monsters," she murmured.

"What did you say?" Vivian reached up and stroked Rachel's hair.

"Monsters," Rachel replied. "You said people turned into monsters because they were so afraid."

"They did." Vivian nodded. "They still do."

Rachel shrugged her mother's hand away from her hair and turned toward the passenger window.

"After today," she said, "I don't see how we're any different from them."

BACK AT THE guesthouse, Vivian pulled the afghan closer around her. Rachel had gone to the greenhouse to check on her orchid seedlings. It was late, but Rachel needed some time alone to think about what she had learned today, so Vivian had let her go. She hoped she had done the right thing in telling her about their involvement in the collaboration. It didn't feel like there was much choice; she had to make Rachel understand the danger.

Vivian wondered if she should have told Rachel *everything*. She had considered it, but Rachel was still so young. And Daniel probably *was* dead, no matter what he had hinted at all those years ago. Vivian hated to think it, but she knew in her heart that any other possibility was slim. Giving Rachel false hope wouldn't serve any purpose. As for today, Vivian didn't see what good it would do to tell Rachel more about the Identification than she already knew.

She tried to drift off to sleep, but her mind kept wandering toward the past. Toward Daniel. To those days in Ganivar, when Rachel was just a baby and Vivian was a frightened young wife hoping that her husband would return from the war.

THEY SENT THE death notice long after Vivian already knew he was gone. She had not received a netcomm for nearly a month, though she checked their account every day. The last vocall, three weeks before, had been odd. Daniel's voice was forced; though he was trying to convey a tone of casual cheer, it rang false. Their streamer was equipped to receive video, but there was no feed from his end, so Vivian couldn't see his face.

"They're sending a group of us across the border tomorrow to reconnoiter a camp that's supposed to be nearby. At the Line."

"Across the border? Where?" she asked, even though she knew it was pointless. Daniel wasn't allowed to be too specific about where he was or what he was doing. "*What camp?*"

"Think." Daniel was silent after uttering that single word. She'd missed something; he was trying to tell her that. Vivian forced herself to concentrate, though she felt like screaming instead. *The Line.* He'd said "the Line." The most controversial section of the National Border Defense System. North, somewhere north of Bensen. Where the Others . . . oh!

"Okay." Vivian said nothing else, hoping he knew she had understood. The artificial tenor of Daniel's voice finally activated some connection in her brain, and she felt tiny electrical explosions of fear going off in her head.

"You understand?"

"Yes." She knew what he had been trying to convey, knew that it should bring her some hope, but all she felt was despair.

"It's an odd bunch, I have to tell you," he said. "The funny thing is, we all have so much in common, this group they've chosen to go. Same types of backgrounds, hell, even the same kinds of hobbies." Daniel laughed, the most horrifying sound she had ever heard, because it was so far removed from what his real laugh sounded like. Vivian stopped breathing, frozen in place at the kitchen counter. The clock on the table flipped from 5:45 to 5:46.

"Viv? Are you there?"

Vivian said nothing. Daniel and she had joked sometimes in college, where they met, about their then-budding
collaboration involvement. They called it their "hobby," as if
it were something they did for fun, just to pass the time. As
if being found with a single meeting notice or having a conversation where the wrong things were said to the wrong
person couldn't get them picked up by an official transport
and driven away, never to be seen on campus again. It had
happened to people. People they knew.

"Viv?" Daniel's voice drew her back to the present.

"I'm here, Daniel." Vivian inhaled, a deep breath, and
straightened her shoulders.

"Did you hear me?"

"Yes, I heard you. I heard you. I . . ."

Tears had been streaming silently down Vivian's face, but
the sob still caught her unawares, and she was sure Daniel
heard it. She gasped, willing herself under control. She could
not let him fear for her, not now. "I love you, Daniel," she
whispered, then louder, "I love you so much."

There was silence. Then his voice again, cracking, but
there, warm in her ear. "I love you too, Viv. I love you more
than I can tell you. I wish . . . I wish I could see you." He
stopped for a minute, and she could hear his breathing.
"Listen to me now. When I get back, we should take a vacation, just get away from it all, what do you say?" He paused
and then continued, emphasizing each word he said. "Get
out of the city. How does that sound, Viv? Get away from
the city."

There was noise around him, some sort of scuffle. Static, and then two more words, the last words she ever heard Daniel say. "*Now*, Viv." The connection broke.

VIVIAN HAD TRIED so hard to forget that day. Having to tell Rachel the truth about Daniel and her being collaborators had brought it all back. And the Identification had forced her to rethink being anywhere near Bensen. Because Vivian had recognized that red coat. The coat the woman who had been Identified had been wearing. It was a coat of a slightly more stylish cut than most women in Bensen wore. She knew it had been expensive, and she knew the woman wearing it had purchased it on impulse, long ago, during a happier time.

Vivian knew that, because she had been with the woman when she bought it.

She watched the door to the guesthouse, waiting for Rachel's return.

CHAPTER 10

ELIZABETH WAS TIDYING up for the night; rinsing her wine-glass in the sink, folding the velvet throw she had covered her legs with while she read her nightly poetry in the parlor. Tonight it had been Ashling's collection of loss sonnets. So much beauty in her words—pain transformed into grace. Elizabeth was in a dreamy state, repeating a particularly heartrending verse in her mind, when she heard the entry chimes. Jonathan's voice scratched over the intercom before she had time to wonder who would be at her door at this hour. She hurried to let him in, worried that his unusual visit might mean something had gone wrong at the greenhouse.

He shuffled a bit on the porch, holding his hat in his hands, obviously uncomfortable. Elizabeth looked at him quizzically for a moment. "Is there some sort of emergency, Jonathan?"

"No," he said, "no emergency, Ms. Moore. At least not yet."

This reply, combined with his odd behavior, made Elizabeth curious. Jonathan rarely came to the house anymore—

hadn't for years—and he never came after hours. They kept their conversations limited to greenhouse business, perhaps the occasional news from town, but nothing more than that. It was an unspoken rule between them, something Jonathan had established all those years ago, and to which Elizabeth adhered willingly. At first she thought it made their continued association less painful for him, but she had since come to believe that it was his way of drawing a line, of telling her that her family and her choices had only so much power over him. She had kept it up regardless of his reasons. It was easier for her.

Once she had determined there was no emergency, Elizabeth told him to come in off the doorstep. He followed her to the parlor, where she offered him wine, which he refused.

"Well," Elizabeth said, "what seems to be the problem, Jonathan?" She motioned for him to sit down; her leg was aching, and she needed to sit herself.

"I was in town today to pick up that load of fertilizer," he said, "and I happened on an Identification."

This *was* news. It had been . . . well, a long time since the last Identification in Bensen. The government avoided the backwaters for the most part, and Bensen was as sleepy as they came. Elizabeth still didn't understand why this would bring Jonathan to her door though.

"Did you know the person Identified, Jonathan?"

"Of course not." Jonathan shot her a look that made it clear he objected to the idea he might have associated with someone who was Identified. "Some woman."

It was not her he wanted to tell Elizabeth about.

"I saw Ms. Quillen and Rachel there, leaving a shop. Sneaking away." Jonathan whispered his next words. "Like criminals would."

"Sneaking away?" Elizabeth frowned. "Surely you're mistaken. Perhaps they were simply in a hurry."

"No, ma'am," Jonathan said, adamant. "They were trying to get out of there unseen, no doubt about it. They were creeping along the walls, slipping along all scared. They scooted round the corner like they were being whipped." Jonathan looked up at her then, and there was something eerily familiar to her about his expression. "There's no reason for upstanding citizens to be scared of the government, and they were scared. I know the girl is probably blameless—she has to do what her mother says, but still. I think it's trouble. I think it could be dangerous for you to keep them on." He was silent a moment. "There's been enough trouble on The Property. Best to avoid any more."

His tone and his audacity angered Elizabeth. That he would even hint at the past's troubles made her furious.

"I am quite capable of determining what is *best*, Jonathan." Her voice was low, but he must have heard the fire in it, for he rushed to assure her that he meant no offense.

"I didn't want to upset you, Ms. Moore. I just thought you should know what you're dealing with."

"I believe I know that quite clearly." Elizabeth's clipped words dismissed him. "Now, if you will show yourself out, Jonathan." She didn't get up.

Hours later she was still sitting where he left her. What Jonathan said *had* upset her, but not in the ways he thought it would. She had been thinking about the world. Thinking about people, and how they could be so certain they knew what they were "dealing with." Thinking about what was truly dangerous.

She couldn't get the picture of Jonathan out of her mind, how he looked when he said he thought there was trouble; that those two poor souls—a widow and a child—might be dangerous. He reminded her then of her grandfather.

She had few memories of her grandfather; she was a little girl when he died. One of the most vivid was of him puttering in the greenhouse. He had long since retired from any daily work there; her father had taken over day-to-day operations shortly after he married Elizabeth's mother. But her grandfather would still fuss with special cross-pollinations, just to "keep up," as he said.

Often he would stare out the greenhouse windows beyond the Line, toward Away. He watched it the way an exhausted rabbit watches wolves making their final approach, glazed past wariness into a sort of trance. When one of the green house workers or Elizabeth's grandmother interrupted his reverie, he would shake his head almost imperceptibly and nod toward the Line. "Worth every cred that thing costs," he would say, "every last one." He never spoke of what it was he feared, what it was he thought the Line was keeping out.

Tonight Jonathan's eyes had looked like her grandfather's did then: full of fear, searching for some unknown danger he was certain lurked in the darkness, just beyond the dim light of his own understanding.

CHAPTER 11

RACHEL HAD BEEN sitting in the greenhouse over an hour, waiting for she didn't know what, watching the sun set, and thinking about her father. She did check her seedlings; they were a special cross she had germinated all by herself. She thought they might be beautiful if they lived. She *knew* they would be unique—something that had never existed before she made them. But she hadn't really come to check on the seedlings. She had come to see if anyone might really be out there, somewhere near the greenhouse, waiting for help.

It was different being in the greenhouse at night. The glass between her and the Line seemed less solid; it sort of disappeared in the dark. It was quiet too; the silence in the shadows around her was deeper somehow than it was in daylight. Even the orchids seemed to radiate a strange luminescence. Rachel felt like she was sitting in some kind of alien garden.

Earlier she had played the corder message back a few times, but she couldn't get any more out of it than she did that morning. Just that whoever it was needed help, and that they would wait near the edge of *something* at sunset. Her eyes were getting achy from staring out past the Line, and it was hard to see anything clearly. She thought she had seen something right before the sun disappeared—a flicker of light in the distance—but there hadn't been anything more.

She hoped her mother was okay. She had seemed better by the time Rachel left for the greenhouse. At least she hadn't been crying anymore. Rachel knew Vivian was worried about her, but she thought, considering everything, that she was fine. Now that she had had a chance to think about things, the fact that her parents were collaborators actually made her feel better. She had always wondered how her mother could be so anti-government and yet so proud of her dad for going to fight some stupid war that the U.S. probably deserved to lose.

She had read everything she could find on the war with Samarik since she was little, trying to find out if there was any way her dad might have survived. Even though most of the records she read were filled with propaganda and double-talk put out by the U.S., it still sounded to her like they were actually the bad guys. She had never known how to feel about the fact that her own father had been a part of something that seemed so obviously wrong.

Her parents' collaboration also explained why Vivian

was so scared all of the time. She tried to hide it, but it still showed; all her warnings about staying low profile in town and keeping their business private and avoiding any trouble. The way she watched what Rachel researched on the streamer. She said she wanted Rachel to think for herself, so it had always seemed strange that she was so strict about Rachel's site visits. Vivian always cautioned her to use a fake screen name if she entered a site that required registration, and any sort of chat room was totally off-limits.

Rachel used to think Vivian was worried that she would stumble upon some porn site, but now she realized that her mother had been worried about tracking. There were government agencies where people sat all day counting up hits on unapproved sites, flagging names for follow-up if they appeared too many times. The streamer at the guesthouse was in Ms. Moore's name, but Rachel could have easily slipped up and mentioned her own name.

Vivian must have wanted to be certain that the name Quillen didn't show up on any lists. There was probably a file on them floating around somewhere. She wondered how long it took before something like that was marked inactive. She wondered if she was in it.

Her mom was always saying how important it was to stand up for what you believe, how injustice must be fought, but today, when injustice was right in front of her, she ran. Rachel didn't see what good all the talk about justice was if nobody tried to help when things got risky. Maybe they couldn't have done anything today, but she felt like they should have at least *tried*. It was hard to believe her mother had once been a collaborator. She didn't seem . . . brave enough.

One thing Rachel knew for sure was that she would never go to college if the only way she could get in was to buy a secured admission. After hearing about her father's friend Alex, she would never be able to live with herself if she thought she might be the cause of that happening to someone else. She wasn't sure how she was going to tell Vivian, but she would figure it out.

Rachel didn't know what she would do instead of a Profession. That was a problem. Because Vivian was right about one thing: It was not a good idea to be without a job. She thought about the Labor Pool crew she had seen today, and about those she had seen on other visits to Bensen. They all looked the same. Not just because they wore the gray jumpsuits. Because they all had the same look in their eyes—a blend of fear and numbness. The boy today had seemed a bit more lively than most, but he would get that look soon enough. Rachel never wanted to see that in the mirror staring back at her.

She squinted out at the Line. There was no sign of anything out there. Maybe she should just give up and go in. A part of her really wanted to; she had to admit she was a little scared. Who was it out there? What was she getting herself into? Vivian would definitely be mad if she knew about this.

But Dad. What would Dad have done? Whoever that

was on the corder, he was in trouble. Her dad would have tried to help, she was sure of it. He might have been afraid, but he would have tried. She knew her mom wanted her to stay safe, but she couldn't pretend she never found the corder. She couldn't pretend that someone out there didn't need her help.

Rachel had brought the minibeam from the kitchen in case she had to wait past dark; she figured she could use it to signal to whoever might be out there.

It was definitely dark now. She decided to try it—two flashes—and see if anything happened. If not, she would go back to the guesthouse.

CHAPTER 12

IT HAD BEEN five nights of waiting. Pathik had been careful to track the time on his trekker, a length of twine with beads on it, knotted at either end. Each night at sunset he had trapped another bead on the "over" side of the string. He remembered when his grandfather, Indigo, had given him his first trekker, on the eve of his first trek alone.

"THIS IS A day, let us say it is *this* day, the day before your first trek," his grandfather had said, holding one of the beads between his fingers. "Until night this day is open, it is free." Grandfather had slithered the bead back and forth on the twine of the trekker, smiling his sly smile. "Anything can happen." Then he slid the bead all the way over to the end of the twine, snug against the end knot. "But soon it is evening, like now. The sun is setting on the day. Each night when this happens, you take a bead, a day, and trap it, like so." He tied a knot on the other side of the bead, so it was held in place on the twine. "And now that day is over. It is frozen, Pathik, finished. It is unchangeable."

Malgam, Pathik's father, had rolled his eyes. "It's a way to track your time, Pathik, to remind you how long you've been out. Not a philosophical lesson." He shook his head at Indigo, but his expression was indulgent, not angry. Pathik was relieved; there would be no arguing that night.

"Just remember, Pathik." His grandfather held the trekker up by the bead he had trapped and flicked the other end with his finger, making the loose beads fly up and down on the twine. "As long as the sun has not set on a day, anything can happen." Malgam exhaled a dramatic sigh, and Indigo laughed, reached across the small fire to muss his son's hair. "Always the practical one, Malgam," he said.

"Somebody has to be, don't they, Da?" Malgam reached into his pack, withdrew his spare knife. "Speaking of practical," he said, "I think you'll probably need this." He tossed the knife to Pathik, who barely caught it, stunned at the casualness of his father's action. Knives were hard to come by, at least real knives, from before. Malgam's spare was a good knife; steel blade, sturdy handle. Pathik tilted it so the blade caught the light of the fire, traced the edge with his finger. He looked up at his father, who was studying him from beneath his hat brim, gauging his reaction. "Take care of it, Pathik," he said. "I can't give you another one." Pathik felt something then, something tight, coming from his father. He was worried, Pathik thought, worried about the trek. First treks could be dangerous; more than one adolescent had not returned to base camp.

"I'll be fine, Da." Pathik slid the knife into his own pack. "Thanks."

They spent the rest of that evening quietly, two men and a boy (though Pathik *felt* quite manly, since he was going on his first solo trek in the morning) gathered around a small campfire, each with his own thoughts, each tied to the others in the tenuous ways that had become all that was left, Away, of family—all that might be left of anything, really.

TO PATHIK, HUDDLED now in the strange field he had been camped near for six days, that first trek seemed like it had happened ages ago. He had been on many since then, foraging for firewood, hunting, looking for better base camp sites. None of his other treks had had so vital a purpose though. Nor had any taken him this close to the Line. Kinec and Jab, his companions on this trek, didn't like its proximity at all; both had refused, after the first night, to journey to the stand of oaks where Pathik waited now. Instead, they had remained at the camp by the stream.

That first night the sight of the house made entirely of glass, something they had all heard stories about since they were little, seemed to unnerve them. Indigo had explained that the building was called a green house, that the glass allowed the sun's warmth to provide a perfect environment for the orchids Indigo said grew inside. But Pathik had always secretly wondered if it was just one of Indigo's stories.

"It's real," Jab had whispered that first night, staring at the structure.

"It's just a building," Pathik had retorted, though he too was awed by the sight of the house, all the glass intact, gleaming in the moonlight. He had heard about this house on many evenings, when they were all tired from a day of hunting, or hauling water to the corn plants, or stacking wood. It was a part of a favorite fire tale told by his grandfather—and here it was, come to life. Jab and Kinec had exchanged glances, not convinced by Pathik's facade of nonchalance. The reality of the glass house made them think of other fire tales, not so happy as that one. If this house actually existed, then those other, far more frightening fire tales might be true as well.

It had taken them four days to reach the stream, and they didn't find the place where it disappeared into the ground until midmorning on the fifth day. It was just as Indigo had described it—one moment the stream was flowing lazily along; the next it was gone, replaced by marshy grassland. It looked like magic until you examined the area and saw the lush growth that indicated the stream's continued course beneath the earth. The group had set up camp there.

Pathik had not even removed his bedroll from his shoulders before he took the corder from his pack. He had carried it as far as he could; it, and the message his grandfather had spoken into it, would have to reach their destination now without his help. He set it on the water, holding it in the slow current for a moment before releasing it. The corder sank, then rose to float a fraction of an inch beneath the surface, moving at a leisurely pace away from him. Within seconds it had disappeared under the earth. He ignored the doubtful looks of Jab and Kinec, though he did whisper to himself, "I hope you are right, Grandfather." To the others, in a louder voice, he said, "Now we wait."

Each night after that first, Pathik left the camp alone at dusk and made his way to the meadow by the Line. He crouched near the oak trees and waited, staring at the glass house, feeling for some sign, though he knew he was too far from the structure to pick up anything. As often as he dared, he lit his lantern and held it up over his head for a few seconds, before snuffing it to conserve the oil. He was painfully aware of the time that had passed. He worried over how long it had taken them to get here, how long it was taking to make contact. He kept thinking about how ill his father, Malgam, had been when they left on this journey.

Each time dawn began to lighten the sky in the meadow, Pathik trudged back to Jab and Kinec, shook his head at their questioning looks, and fell into his bedroll to sleep. Five times now, and it looked like this night's end would make six. Jab and Kinec were ready to go back. They had told him so that morning. Kinec had spoken, while Jab shuffled behind him.

"One more night, Pathik." Kinec had sounded firm. "If nothing happens tonight, we go back after you've had some sleep. Midmorning tomorrow we need to be on our way."

Jab had chimed in then. "We don't even know if anyone found the corder. For all we know, we are waiting for nothing and your father is already dead. It's—" Jab stumbled sideways from the elbow Kinec shoved into his ribs but finished his complaint. "It's too dangerous." He glared at Kinec, then at Pathik. "We need to get back." Pathik had said nothing. He was tired. He knew that Jab might be right.

Pathik slept, and when he awoke, he huddled with the others around the tiny fire they had built. They shared some of the dried meat they had brought, but no one talked. After a bit Pathik got up and fetched the lantern and his jacket. When he was ready to leave for the meadow, he turned back, looked at both of them. "We'll go tomorrow. If nothing happens tonight, we'll leave when I get back." He walked away without waiting to hear what they said.

So there he sat, waiting in a strange meadow. They had been gone from home for too long. Pathik wondered if the others were right, if his father was already dead. He lit the lantern and held it up, watching the glass house to see if anyone acknowledged his signal. Nothing, just like the night before. He sat back down and snuffed the lantern, took his trekker from his pocket, and selected the top bead from the loose ones on the end. He slid it back and forth on the twine. "Anything can happen," he said, under his breath, and smiled. Grandfather. His hair was completely gray now, trimmed short, though Pathik could remember when it was still more dark than gray, dark and long. Even now his eyes still held their sparkle, those blue, blue eyes. Pathik had the same eyes, and he took some teasing for it from Nandy.

"You'll be the end of some sweet thing's heart, Pathik," she liked to tell him. "If your da had those eyes, it wouldn't have taken me so long to get over his crusty old personality. I would have swooned!" Nandy usually did a little act then, holding her hands together against her cheek and leaning far over to one side, her eyes closed, laughing. Malgam laughed too, though he always tried to swat her. Nandy had made a difference in him. He was less angry now that she was a part of their family. Pathik wondered what she was doing right now, this moment. He looked around at the dark field and snorted. "Sleeping, you foolishness," he muttered to himself, "like you should be."

He slid the bead he'd been playing with over to the other side of his trekker and knotted it in place. "Trapped," he whispered to himself. "Over."

If Pathik hadn't been so tired, he probably would have cried.

Then he saw the light.

CHAPTER 13

RACHEL FOUND HERSELF at the place next to the Line where she had tried to Cross—it seemed so long ago—without being conscious of having left the greenhouse or of walking to the spot. She peered into the dark, unable to see anything past a few feet. She was shaking. The moment she had seen the glow in the distance—such a soft, strange light, briefly glimmering and then eclipsed—her body had begun to tremble.

It was real. Somebody was *out there.*

She stood waiting, trying to breathe calmly. She listened intently, but there was no sound. She flashed the minibeam twice and listened more. There was nothing. The night was still.

Then she heard it. A faint rustle of grass, just once, somewhere straight ahead of her. She squinted into the distance but saw nothing. Another rustling, to the left this time, closer. A denser darkness rose there, shambling forward. Rachel couldn't discern anything but movement for a long time. She held her breath, listening as the sounds got nearer. Slowly, a form began to take shape—a human form. It was extraordinary to see it, out in the meadow where nothing had ever been but birds and trees, on the *other* side of the Line.

At first, Rachel couldn't tell if it was a man or a woman. As the distance between them narrowed, she could see through the gloom of twilight that it was neither. It was a boy, about her age. She could tell that he saw her—he was walking straight toward her. He came to a halt three feet away from her. He seemed unwilling to get too close to the Line.

They stared at each other for a time, eyes wide.

"Hello." He spoke quietly, and she was somehow surprised that the sound of a voice could penetrate the barrier of the Line, though she had often heard the birds singing beyond it.

"Hello," she whispered. She could make out tousled brown hair. He was taller than she was, and very lean. But he looked no different than any boy in Bensen, really, except for the way he was dressed. He wore a shirt and pants made of some thick, rough fabric. They had no ornamentation of any kind, unless you counted the buttons down the front of the shirt. He carried what looked like a jacket crumpled under one arm. In his hand was a lantern, made of real glass surrounded by a rusty metal framework. Rachel flicked on the minibeam and adjusted it to the brightest setting.

"Turn that thing off!" The boy dropped as if he had been shot. "Do you want us both dead?"

Rachel fumbled with the switch and extinguished the light.

"Sorry." She felt bad for being careless, but at the same time she didn't care for his tone. Pretty bossy for someone who needed her help. "I just wanted to see better."

The boy stayed low to the ground, looking all around in a way that reminded Rachel of an animal, sniffing the air. Finally, he stood up again, scowling. "Yeah. Well . . . not a good idea." He brushed off his pants and picked up the lantern he had dropped.

"My name is Pathik," he said.

"Rachel."

Each seemed to be stunned at the fact of the other, standing just a few feet apart, yet separated by so much more than that few feet. Rachel wished she could turn on the minibeam and see him more clearly.

"I got your message," Rachel said. She kept her voice low.

"Indigo said you would."

"Who is Indigo?"

Pathik looked troubled. "He thought you might know."

"Was he the voice on the corder? Half the message was gone." Rachel watched, fascinated, as Pathik turned his head this way and that again, sniffing. He cast about as though he was trying determine the source of some odor. "What are you doing?"

Pathik ignored her question. "I think we should sit." He lowered himself to the ground in one smooth motion.

"Look, I don't know how long I can stay out here," Rachel said, sitting down. "My mom will be worrying. So you better fill me in, if you can. I know somebody needs help. But that's about all I know." Her voice sounded normal, but her heart was beating awfully fast. One of the *Others* was close enough that she could touch his knee if she stretched a bit. Well, she could have if the Line wasn't between them. She could see Pathik's chest move when he breathed. She could hear the lantern's handle clink against the glass when he set it down. It seemed like there was nothing separating them. Yet some part of Rachel was glad the Line was there. Pathik *looked* like a normal boy, but she felt something she couldn't identify coming from him. Something mesmeric, that she didn't like. It felt dangerous.

"Indigo is my grandfather." Pathik spoke so quietly that Rachel had to lean toward him to hear. "He sent me here to get help. My father is sick. Indigo has been caring for him, but he can do no more. My father may be . . ." Pathik's voice broke. "He may be dying. Others have died from this sickness."

Rachel frowned. "If your father is that sick, why haven't you taken him to a doctor? I mean, have you? Is Indigo a doctor? Why—"

"We have no doctors." Pathik looked angry. "You say you don't have much time, right? So why don't you listen instead of talking."

Rachel's retort was in her throat, but she let it die there. "I'm listening," she said.

Pathik looked down for a moment. Rachel thought she saw the shimmer of tears before he ducked his head, but when he looked back up, his eyes were dry.

"Indigo says Father needs medicine that we don't have. He called it Anti-biotics. He said to come here and try to get it." The expression on his face was one of hope suppressed. Rachel recognized it right away. Later she would wonder why; there was nothing so desperate in her own life that his expression should seem so familiar, was there?

In the present moment what she felt was happiness. She was about to make a difference. She could help this boy, and no one could tell her to stop it.

"I can get antibiotics for you." She beamed at Pathik. "I know where some are."

Pathik sniffed the air.

"What is that?" Rachel felt irritated. She had just told the boy she could help him save his father and all he could do was sniff. "What are you doing when you do that?"

He looked at her for a long time before he answered. He seemed to be weighing something in his mind. Rachel wondered if he was considering whether to kill her. She hoped she hadn't been foolish to think of the Line as protection. She knew nothing about this boy.

She actually flinched when he finally replied, as though his words were a blow. She hoped he didn't notice.

"I'm feeling," he said, watching her face. "I can feel . . .

emotion. If it's strong, and if it's close enough. I can sense if someone is happy or angry or even lying. People feel afraid when they're lying, a certain kind of afraid."

Rachel was impressed. It wasn't as interesting as a cat the size of a sheep or someone shooting flames from their eyes, but it was something. Something Otherly.

"So do you think I'm lying? About getting the medicine?"

"I know you're not." Pathik smiled. He looked so different in that moment, not frightening at all. Rachel felt that vague pull again and unconsciously shifted backward.

"Well, then . . . Oh." Rachel looked stricken. "Oh no."

"What?" Pathik's smile dimmed.

"It doesn't matter," Rachel said. "It doesn't matter if I can get the antibiotics. I can't get them *to* you." She pointed at the Line.

"I have that under control." Pathik's smile returned, full strength. He looked around, and for a moment Rachel thought he was going to start his sniffing again. Instead, he got up and walked a few feet along the Line, stopping at a large rock that was half buried in the ground. Rachel watched as he took a metal rod of some sort from his jacket pocket. It looked like part of an old, broken tool. It was flattened on one end, and Pathik used it to dig in the soil at the base of the rock. He dug fast, and in no time he had excavated a deep, narrow hole. From it, he withdrew a small, battered box, which he set on the ground with near reverence. He refilled the hole he had made, smoothed the dirt a bit, and returned with the box to where Rachel waited.

"This will disable the Line," he said, sitting down near her again. He held the box out to Rachel so she could see its contents as he opened it. "A key." He watched her face.

Rachel peered into the box, excited and nervous. What would the key look like? How would it work?

Her eyes must have given it away. She didn't even have time to look up at him before Pathik had withdrawn the box to see for himself.

It was empty.

Pathik opened his mouth, but no sound came out. He dug his fingers around the inside of the box, held it upside down and shook it. Finally, he dropped it on the ground in front of him. His head sank down, as though he had no more energy left in his body. Rachel wondered how far he had come to find this. An empty box.

"No key," she said.

Pathik raised his head then, his eyes blazing at her. "Just get the medicine. If you get the medicine, I will find a way."

"I'll get it." Rachel was more than a little frightened of him at that moment, but she also felt awful for him. "I'll get it. I'll bring it tomorrow night."

He exhaled, as though he had been holding his breath until she answered. He nodded, still looking into her eyes. "Thank you."

CHAPTER 14

VIVIAN HUMMED SOFTLY to keep herself awake while she dusted the parlor, a tune she remembered Daniel whistling when they walked together on Sunday mornings. Before Rachel. Before . . . before a lot of things. "Our gamboling," Daniel had called it. They never had a destination; they would set out from the apartment and walk where they pleased. They would usually end up at some café, sharing a pastry and laughing at nothing. Daniel's eyes had crinkled at the corners when he laughed.

Something was going on with Rachel, something more than her being troubled by the revelations about her father. She had been out until very late last night, though Vivian knew that she hadn't been far. Where was there to go, really, on The Property? Vivian had gone to bed after Rachel left to go check on her seedlings, but she was restless. When Rachel had still not returned after darkness fell, Vivian had finally roused herself and padded in her bare feet down the moonlit path to the greenhouse. She saw no sign of Rachel at first, and she had begun to worry. Then she saw a minibeam light playing on the meadow beyond the greenhouse. She traced the path of the beam back to the greenhouse.

Rachel was sitting inside the potting room in the dark, holding the light. Vivian didn't call out. She thought it might be best to let the poor girl think things through. Instead, she watched as Rachel clicked the minibeam on and off, wondering how she could help her daughter make some sense of things, now that she knew the truth of it. After a few moments she turned and headed back to bed. Hours later she heard Rachel come in, heard her slide carefully into the cot where she had slept since she was four. That was the year she had declared herself "too growed up" to share a bed with her mother. Vivian had been able to sleep then.

But this morning she was worried again. There had been something familiar about that moment in the moonlight last night, about the minibeam clicking on and off, on and off. Something Vivian didn't like.

"Ms. Quillen."

Vivian stifled a yawn as she turned to face Ms. Moore, who had entered the room.

"Ms. Moore. I was just finishing up in here." Vivian smoothed her hair back, eyeing the strict perfection of Ms. Moore's bun. "Did you have any special requests for the market today, ma'am? I was going to finalize the list for next week."

Ms. Moore sat down in one of the chairs near the fireplace. She stroked the fabric on the chair arm for a moment.

Then she looked up at Vivian. "You look tired this morning, Ms. Quillen. Come sit down for a moment."

"Oh, I'm fine, Ms. Moore." Vivian folded her dusting cloth in half, then in quarters. "I had a bit of trouble getting to sleep last night, but I'm fine."

Ms. Moore smiled faintly. She pointed to the other chair near the fire. "Actually," she said, "I wanted to speak with you. Briefly." Her left eyebrow raised a half inch. "If you have the time?"

Vivian returned Ms. Moore's look for a beat, then moved to the second chair, still clutching her dusting cloth. She sat on the edge of the chair. "Is there something wrong, Ms. Moore?"

"Oh, I should hope not," said Ms. Moore mildly, watching Vivian's face. "I should hope there is not." She smoothed the arm of the chair again, petting it as though it were a cat. "I wonder, Ms. Quillen, if everything is all right with you? I wonder if there has been anything troubling you lately?"

Vivian's chest tightened. She stared intently at her hands strangling the dusting cloth in her lap, willing them to relax around it. "I'm not sure I know what you mean, Ms. Moore," she said, her voice cool. "Everything is fine."

Silence rose up between the two women, drawing a lazy line from one pair of eyes to the other. The air seemed to grow still. Vivian held Ms. Moore's gaze calmly, steeling herself inside. Then, before she could stop herself, she yawned. The dusting cloth fluttered in her hands as she tried, too late, to cover her mouth.

"That," Ms. Moore said, politely looking away, "for instance. I don't believe I have ever seen you look so tired, Ms. Quillen."

"As I said Ms. . . . Ms. . . ." Another yawn struck, and Vivian had to wait for it to end before she could continue. "As I said, just a little trouble sleeping."

"And something else." Ms. Moore looked uncomfortable. "Something that was seen in town."

Alarm flared scarlet in Vivian's mind. She searched Ms. Moore's eyes for some clue of what was coming. She knew better than to speak. She had been through collaborator training after all, and though it was years ago, she did remember a few things. One was *never add to the evidence.* She still remembered the trainer's face; a young face in an old man, at least she had thought so at the time. In truth, he was probably no older than she was now. But at the time, he had seemed ancient to her. His hands had been weathered, much like Jonathan's, and he got up from the sessions with difficulty, as though his joints were painful. It was rumored that his relatively youthful face was due to a backroom laser job years before; he had been "reconfigured" so the authorities couldn't easily spot him. He was born before recording genids became routine at every birth, when changing your appearance might still save you. She remembered his warning during a training session. "If they are trying to dig your grave," he had said, "you don't grab a shovel and help. You sit still and you shut up."

Vivian sat still. She met Ms. Moore's eyes with an

innocent expression. "What do you mean, Ms. Moore?"

Ms. Moore studied her, tilting her head slightly. At last, she spoke.

"Ms. Quillen." Her voice was low, but severe. "I won't dwell on details here, but a source informs me that you and Rachel behaved oddly during your last visit to Bensen. That you behaved in such a manner as to cast suspicion upon yourselves. That . . ."

"Suspicion of *what*, exactly, Ms. Moore?" Vivian's face was almost as red as her hair. "And who, may I ask, is this source?" She stopped herself, taking a deep breath and unclenching her hands. She flattened the wrinkles in the crumpled dust cloth, ironing it with her fingers. Calmer, she began again. "Rachel and I went to Bensen to do the marketing as we always do. If shopping is suspicious, then I guess we were acting suspiciously."

Ms. Moore remained silent, watching. Flustered, Vivian twisted the dust cloth into a tight wad, trying to restrain herself. Her fear got the better of her though, and she spoke. "After all the years I've worked for you, I cannot believe that some mean-spirited gossip from town could make you question me in this way . . ."

"Ms. Quillen!" Vivian was stunned into silence. Ms. Moore *never* raised her voice, and while her interjection could not be called a shout, it was certainly the closest thing to one Vivian had ever heard from her. She waited, afraid to hear what would come next.

Ms. Moore leaned toward Vivian. "Ms. Quillen," she

said, more quietly. "You *have* worked for me for a long time. And you have been a good employee, despite my initial misgivings about you. But there has been no trouble on The Property for many, many years, and I have no wish to see it return." Ms. Moore shook her head. She leaned back in her chair and looked at the fireplace mantel. She stared at it for a long time, so long that Vivian looked too.

The trinkets she saw there were as they always were. The black stone candlesticks, cool to the touch and heavy. The glass box, the porcelain cat figurine, the framed digim. She had dusted and polished these objects so many times, they had become invisible to her in some sense, yet they had grown to represent something to her too—a feeling of familiarity, the sense that she belonged simply because she, like they, had been here so long. Looking at them now, frightened as she was, she felt as though she had never seen them before. They seemed foreign in some way, abstract.

"The source I received my information from is reliable." Ms. Moore's voice startled Vivian out of her reverie. "And I must question you in order to ensure that I am aware of any risk." Ms. Moore scrutinized Vivian's face, searching it for something. "When you came here, Ms. Quillen, so many years ago, as you say, you were in some sort of difficulty. I want to know if that difficulty has arisen again. From what I understand, there were Enforcement Officers in town, and you appeared to be quite reluctant to be noticed by them."

Vivian knew better than to deny *everything*. She hoped she could minimize the damage by admitting to a lesser evil.

"I was . . ." She bowed her head. "I was a bit reckless in my youth, Ms. Moore. I didn't realize how serious things could get. My husband and I dabbled in certain . . . activities we shouldn't have, because we were too young to know better. And once your name is associated with the collab . . . once you have a brush with the authorities, it's hard to forget how harsh they can be. We were marked as troublemakers, and it made our lives very difficult for some time." Vivian stopped for a moment. Her eyes had filled with tears, and she dabbed at them with the dust cloth.

"Ms. Moore, my husband died for this country. I don't think you can ask for a show of loyalty more genuine than that. But I still remember how hard the authorities made it for us because of one mistake. When Rachel and I went to town, we did see an Identification. It made me feel nervous, that's all. I wanted to get as far away from it as I could, as fast as I could. If someone saw us there, they may have misinterpreted my nervousness as some sort of guilt." Vivian met Ms. Moore's look candidly, hoping her explanation was believable.

Ms. Moore sighed. "I am sorry for your loss, Ms. Quillen. I'm sure your husband thought he was doing the right thing." She shook her head again, almost imperceptibly this time. "Given your experience as a youth, I think I understand why you may have wanted to avoid the Enforcement Officers. They can be quite frightening. And we have all made mistakes in our youth." Ms. Moore fell silent, her eyes drifting again to the fireplace mantel. She said nothing for a long time, so long that Vivian began to wonder if she was ill.

"Ms. Moore?" Vivian finally interrupted the older woman's reverie. "Are you all right?"

Ms. Moore turned her head to look at Vivian, but her attention lagged behind her eyes, still occupied in whatever place her mind had visited during her silence. A second passed before she focused on Vivian's face. "I will need your assurance that there is no reason to be alarmed regarding the authorities, Ms. Quillen. As I said, I have no wish for them to become interested in The Property. We have had peace here for many years, and while that may not be much, it is something."

Vivian could feel relief flooding her veins. Still, she replied cautiously. "I have no reason to believe the authorities are interested in me, Ms. Moore. I was foolish in my youth, but I have not been foolish for many years."

"Very well then." Ms. Moore rose slowly from her seat. "I regret any discomfort my inquiry may have caused." She gripped the arm of the chair to help steady herself. "I believe I may retire for an hour or so, Ms. Quillen. I feel a bit worn out. If you could call me for lunch?"

"Of course, Ms. Moore." Vivian arose too, her body still buzzing with a combination of panic and relief. She watched Ms. Moore make her way slowly to the stairs. When the lady was out of sight, she closed her eyes and sagged against her chair, hand on her chest. She leaned there until her breathing had steadied, until she felt she could return to her cleaning.

Vivian spent most of the rest of the day worrying. She worried about Ms. Moore's suspicions, though she thought she might have successfully headed those off, at least for now. She worried even more about Rachel. She kept thinking of the minibeam light from the night before, flicking on and off. She couldn't pinpoint what was bothering her, but she knew she was going to keep a sharp eye on Rachel from now on. Sharper than usual, poor girl.

It wasn't until afternoon, while she was putting the lunch dishes away, that Vivian remembered something Ms. Moore had said. She had remarked that she had no wish to see trouble *return* to The Property. When, Vivian wondered, as she dried the luncheon platter, had trouble been here before?

What kind of trouble had it been?

CHAPTER 15

IT WAS BEGINNING to get dark. Rachel wished Pathik would hurry up. She wasn't sure how long she could stay out tonight. She felt uneasy about Vivian. After dinner Rachel had asked her mom if she could check on her new seedlings once more before bed. Vivian had barely looked up from the streamer; she was watching the local news.

"Okay, sweetie," she had said, stifling a yawn. "Don't be too late. I may go to bed early tonight, but I'll leave a light on for you."

Rachel had hugged her and slipped out the door, wondering how she got off so easily. She had expected Vivian to say no. The night before, Vivian had let her go to the greenhouse without much questioning, but they'd both been upset by the Identification, and the talk they had after it. Rachel figured Vivian's unusual lenience was understandable in those circumstances. But two nights in a row? Rachel didn't like it. She had been ready to cry and carry on and claim that she just needed a little time to think, in order to get permission to go.

But no. Nothing but "Okay, sweetie." Rachel had been thinking about it while she waited in the greenhouse, and it seemed suspicious.

She pointed the minibeam toward the ground and flicked the switch to make sure the charge was good. She didn't want to risk not being able to signal Pathik that it was safe. He might think she hadn't come, that she had been too afraid. Last night she could tell that he thought she was frightened.

Maybe that was true, but right now all she felt was impatience. She wished he would hurry up and get here. She divided her attention between looking for his signal and watching the greenhouse door. The more she thought about Vivian's nonchalance tonight, the more anxious she became.

Getting the antibiotics hadn't been as hard as Rachel thought it would be. Rachel knew where they would be if there were any left. The day after Ms. Moore was hurt, Jonathan had sent Rachel to the house with a dendrobium cutting to put on her breakfast tray. Rachel had watched Vivian take bottles of pills from the cupboard above the sink and remove capsules, which she placed on a cloth napkin next to the glass of orange juice Ms. Moore had every morning. Vivian had told her then that one type of pill was for pain, and the other was to make sure that Ms. Moore's leg didn't get infected. Rachel had gambled on the hope that Ms. Moore hadn't used them all, and she had been right.

This morning Rachel had feigned sleep while Vivian dressed and waited until she heard the front door shut. Then Rachel followed her. She stayed well back on the path so that she wouldn't be seen. She knew that the first thing Vivian would do was to prepare Ms. Moore's tray and take it up to her. Rachel waited outside the kitchen door, hidden in the shrubs.

She listened hard, but she couldn't hear any sounds from inside; no cabinets closing, no dishes clattering. She wondered how she would know that Vivian had gone upstairs. Finally, she crept to the door and crouched under the window in its top half, pressing her ear against the wood beneath. She was about to risk a peek when she heard a buzzer go off inside. The timer! That meant that Ms. Moore's muffins were done. Rachel heard her mother's voice.

"There, now. Ah, these look tasty." Rachel could hear her mom walking back and forth in the kitchen as she gathered the things she needed and placed them on the tray. "All right then, time for breakfast."

Rachel waited until she heard nothing more. She rose up stealthily and peered into the kitchen through the window. It was empty. She took hold of the doorknob and squeezed her eyes shut, praying fervently. "Please be unlocked, please be unlocked, please be unlocked," she whispered to herself. The knob turned easily. As simple as that, she was in the kitchen.

She didn't have time to feel scared. She raced over to the sink and opened the cabinet door above it. There they were, two bottles of brownish plastic, with labels handwritten by Dr. Beller. She grabbed the first bottle and shook it. It was about half full. "Erythromycicillin XVII," she read from the label. Quickly, she opened the bottle and poured all but a few of the red capsules into a bag she pulled from her pocket. She replaced the lid and put the bottle back on the shelf. On impulse, she opened the other bottle. It was practically full of green capsules. Dr. Beller had written "For pain" on its label. Rachel poured half of the capsules into the bag. Then she put the bottle back and ran.

Rachel had brought the capsules with her tonight, though she still didn't know how she would manage to get them to Pathik. She hoped he had found some way to make it possible. She wondered what was taking him so long. Maybe he wasn't coming. Maybe he thought she hadn't been able to get the medicine. Worse, maybe he thought she hadn't even tried. When she told him she thought she could get him the medicine his father needed, he had seemed so hopeful. But there was something in his face that made her think he doubted her.

Finally, Rachel saw a glow in the meadow. It was him, signaling as they had agreed. She raised the minibeam and clicked it on and off twice to let him know it was safe to come forward.

She watched as he approached, first nothing more than a dark shape in the field, then more plainly a human, then unmistakably Pathik, standing in front of her in his odd clothes, sniffing the air like a dog. Pathik looked so silly bobbing his head around that she couldn't help but laugh.

"Getting anything really bad?" Rachel said when Pathik was near enough to hear her whisper. "Any bears? Maybe a tiger? Someone from the government?"

Even in the dim light, she could see Pathik's disgusted expression. "It doesn't work that way."

"Yeah, well, whatever." Rachel pulled the bag of pills out of her jacket pocket. She was feeling pretty proud of herself. "I got the stuff," she said. "Now we just have to figure out how to get it from me to you."

Pathik said nothing.

"Well?" Rachel was pretty sure Pathik didn't have a clue how to get the medicine across the Line. "Any solutions to our little problem?"

Pathik was busy sniffing.

"Oh, come on." Rachel was about to make a snide comment about psychic noses when Pathik held up his hand to silence her. He stared at her, and for the first time Rachel noticed how blue his eyes were—a deep, soft blue. They seemed, right now, to be emanating a light of their own. Suddenly that light disappeared as Pathik's face dropped from sight.

"Rachel!" Vivian's strained whisper reached Rachel's ears at the same time she felt her mother's hand close around her wrist. "Come with me." Vivian yanked at Rachel hard, whirling her around. "I knew it," she hissed. "I knew it was a signal, just like Daniel and Peter used to do on maneuvers with other collaborators. The minute I saw that minibeam, I should have stopped you." Vivian started toward the greenhouse with Rachel in tow, her hand wrapped in a death grip around Rachel's wrist.

"Mom!" Rachel struggled to free herself from her mother's hold, digging her feet into the dirt. "Let go of me!"

"Quiet." Vivian's voice was a low growl. Rachel had never seen her like this, not even in Bensen when they were trying to get away from the Identification without being noticed.

"Rachel." Vivian lifted Rachel's chin with her free hand, forcing Rachel to look her in the eye. "Keep your voice down and get moving. There is no time right now to argue."

"But Mom!" Rachel threw herself to the ground, using the same technique she had used when she was five years old and didn't want to go where her mother told her. Now that she weighed as much as Vivian did, it actually worked. "I have to help Pathik. Indigo said we would help! Pathik's father is *dying*, Mom. I can't just pretend that isn't happening!" Rachel glared up at her mother. "Dad wouldn't have!" She spat the words out at Vivian, surprised at the venom she felt toward her.

"Your dad is gone!" Vivian crouched over her, still holding her wrist, her face close to Rachel's. She stared at her daughter, her breath coming in gasps. When she spoke again, her voice was tight, each word carefully pronounced. "I am not discussing this with you now, Rachel. You have no idea what you're risking, what can happen to you. Just get up *now* and move. We cannot afford any trouble."

"Nor can I." Rachel and Vivian turned simultaneously

at the sound of Ms. Moore's voice. She was standing in the middle of the flattened path of grass that Rachel's feet had formed during her trips back and forth from the greenhouse. She was wearing a long bed robe, and her hair was, for the second time ever, a mess, steel strands flying loose around her head. She was aiming a stunner straight at the two of them.

"That's illegal." Vivian, frozen in a half crouch over Rachel, could not seem to take her eyes off the stunner in Ms. Moore's hand. "Civilians aren't allowed to carry weapons." Her voice wavered, and she looked as shocked as if she had just seen Ms. Moore break into a tap dance on the parlor table.

Ms. Moore made a sound between a snort and a chuckle. "Civilians aren't allowed much these days, are they, Ms. Quillen?" She lowered the stunner, carefully pointing the laser end away from her feet. "I thought I might need this to help convince you to leave The Property. All this sneaking around at night has me convinced that you *are* trouble, after all, more trouble than I can afford to have here." She raised an eyebrow in response to Rachel's astonished look. "Do you think I am totally unaware of what goes on here on my own property, young lady? I've had reason to pay particular attention of late, even if I've been assured that there is no cause for concern." She shot Vivian a look. "However, from what I've just overheard, this trouble may be my own."

Something in Ms. Moore's eyes changed when she said this, and her face transformed from stern to sad. She turned to Rachel. "You said the name Indigo." Ms. Moore looked into Rachel's eyes intently, as though they might reveal something important. "Who is that?"

"Pathik's grandfather," Rachel whispered, staring back at Ms. Moore. "He told Pathik we would help. Pathik's father is dying . . ." She held out the bag of pills she had stolen. "He *needs* these." Rachel opened the bag to show Ms. Moore its contents. "I took them from your kitchen. I was going to give them to Pathik—there was supposed to be some way to shut down the Line. But it wasn't there, and . . ." Rachel couldn't go on. Her face was burning, and her throat felt like it was going to close up.

Ms. Moore took a deep breath. She touched the ring hanging from the chain around her neck, her gaze lowered to the ground. "Indigo," she whispered, as though she were confiding a secret to the grass. She looked back up at Rachel. "Where," she said, "is this Pathik?"

Rachel began to get up off the ground. Vivian, who had been silent during the exchange between her employer and her daughter, helped her up. They looked at each other, and Vivian gave an almost imperceptible nod. Rachel pointed behind her toward the Line. "He's right there," she said.

The three of them turned to look where Rachel was pointing. The path of flattened grass Rachel had made led up to a place right next to the Line. On the other side, a similar trodden path approached the same spot.

No one was there.

Ms. Moore walked right up to the Line, the closest she

had been to it in years, and spoke. She said she thought she knew what the boy needed to get the medicine across. She told him, or perhaps she only told the meadow, that she would try to get it. She asked him to come back in two nights if he could, to that spot. They all waited to see if he would come out from his hiding place, but there was nothing. Ms. Moore stared into the dark for a long time. Then she turned back to Rachel and Vivian.

"Come to the house with me now. I have some things to tell you."

CHAPTER 16

RACHEL SAT ON the sofa. Vivian was seated on one of the sentry chairs across from her. They were both wide-eyed, stunned. Ms. Moore came in from the kitchen with a tray, upon which were three glasses and a decanter of wine.

"It's time we all had a frank chat." Ms. Moore served the wine calmly, as though she were hosting an evening social. Rachel couldn't stop staring at her. She seemed so unruffled. But she was wearing a *robe*. With a stunner poking out of one pocket. And her hair was *messy*.

"The man in that digim"—Ms. Moore pointed to the mantel—"is Indigo." She looked at Rachel. "Apparently, your Pathik is his grandson."

Rachel gasped. She stared at Ms. Moore, and then at the digim. "But that man is so young," she said.

"He was then," said Ms. Moore. "That was years ago, before you were even born, Rachel."

"His eyes. Pathik's eyes are the same color. So Indigo

must be his grandfather, don't you think? I've never seen eyes that color on anyone else." Rachel looked at Ms. Moore and Vivian for confirmation.

Ms. Moore sat down in the empty sentry chair. She reached for her glass. Rachel noticed that her hand was shaking. She caught her mom's attention, motioning with her head toward Ms. Moore.

Vivian saw what she meant. "Are you all right, Ms. Moore?"

Ms. Moore set the glass back down on the table without having taken a drink. She looked pale.

"If Pathik *is* Indigo's grandson, that makes him my grandson too."

"What?" Rachel didn't mean for her voice to be quite so loud. "How?"

Ms. Moore held up a hand. "Let me explain it, Rachel." She took a deep breath, then another. She looked as miserable as Rachel had ever seen her look.

"Indigo is one of the Others. He and I were in love. We had a child—Pathik's father—together."

Rachel started to speak again, but Vivian shushed her. Ms. Moore continued.

"Indigo Crossed many, many years ago. I was only a few years older than you, Rachel, when we met. He'd come with a small group of Others, on a mission of some sort. It didn't go well, and his friends were killed. He was very ill himself and unable to Cross back to Away for some time, and . . . well, we met. And we fell in love."

Vivian interrupted. "I don't understand. How did he Cross? The Border Defense System is supposed to be impenetrable."

"I'll get to that." Ms. Moore reached again for her wine. Her hand was still shaking, but she managed to take a sip without spilling.

Rachel had her own question.

"Did you know he was one of them, one of the Others?"

Ms. Moore turned to her. "I did, Rachel. You know how many strangers we see on The Property. It was no different in those days. He tried to tell me he was from town at first, but there was something about him. Something . . . different. I knew he wasn't telling me the truth." She tilted her head, studying Rachel. "Why do you ask that?"

Rachel met Ms. Moore's eyes. She wasn't sure if she should answer honestly, but she did anyway.

"I was betting you didn't. Know, I mean. That he was one of the Others."

"Hmm." Ms. Moore nodded, as though she understood.

"I mean, the Others are supposed to be dangerous, evil. You don't seem to be the type of person who would . . . take chances." Rachel bit her lip, wishing she could take those words back.

Ms. Moore surprised her though. She smiled. Briefly. And then she looked very sad.

"That is so true, Rachel. I'm sure I don't seem like someone who would take such a chance. I haven't taken any real chances in a very long time." Ms. Moore's eyes glittered with unspilled tears. "I regret that in so many ways. But, back then, when I was a young girl, I wasn't like I am now. I was more like you. At least for a while."

"Like me?" Rachel could not imagine Ms. Moore as anything but gray-haired and reserved.

"Yes, like you. You are brave, Rachel. It couldn't have been easy to steal my medicine."

That made Rachel squirm a little. "I'm sorry about that, Ms. Moore. I know it was wrong to take it. It's just . . ."

Ms. Moore waved Rachel's apology away. "Yes, it was wrong, Rachel. Of course, I don't *condone* such behavior, under normal circumstances. But you saw a way to help someone in need, someone most people *would* consider evil, and you did it. It was a brave thing to do."

"She gets that from her father." Vivian smiled at Rachel.

"Well, I used to be like that too. Brave." Ms. Moore took another sip of her wine. "When I met Indigo, I knew *he* wasn't evil. And as we got to know each other, I learned about the Others. Some of them *are* different from us, but they are not evil."

"How do you know they aren't?" Rachel watched Ms. Moore intently.

"Indigo told me what he knew of the Others' history. He grew up hearing the stories about the beginning around their campfires in the evening, when people could rest a bit after the day's work." Ms. Moore looked from Rachel to Vivian and back again. "They are just people, like we are. People who paid a price for events they had nothing to do with. Perhaps you should know some of what he told me about his people. About how history looks to *them*." She settled back in her chair. "Is your mother teaching you about U.S. history, Rachel?"

"I have to study every single—"

"Rachel." Vivian frowned at Rachel and then turned to Ms. Moore. "Yes."

Ms. Moore smiled at Vivian. "Then you both know about how the Line came to be, how people were trapped on the wrong side."

Rachel and Vivian nodded.

"Many of those people died in the initial blast from the bomb Korusal dropped. More people died from the sickness that came in the days after the blast. Those left alive—Indigo's great-grandparents among them—managed to gather together in small groups. The group Indigo's great-grandparents were with numbered a hundred twenty-five souls. At first, they had all they could do to survive.

"They had to learn how to live without the conveniences they had 'before.' That's how history is divided Away: before the Line was activated and after. The survivors struggled to forget the people they had been separated from forever. Some could not forget. Those often disappeared from camp without a word, never to be seen again."

"You mean, nobody went looking for them?" Rachel couldn't believe it.

"No, Rachel." Ms. Moore shook her head softly. "They had no choice, really. There were people hurt and ill, and no food sources after a while. Those that found the will to continue had their hands full. It wasn't like the life you know."

"So the people that left," Rachel whispered. "They probably died."

Ms. Moore nodded silently.

Vivian refilled Ms. Moore's glass.

"Thank you, Ms. Quillen."

"Please. Call me Vivian. If you're comfortable with that."

Ms. Moore looked at Vivian, surprised. Rachel was sure she was going to say something brusque about formalities, but she didn't.

"Well, I suppose you must call me Elizabeth, then."

Rachel gawked. She couldn't believe what she'd just heard. Ms. Moore looked at her and laughed softly.

"You, young lady, shall continue to address me as Ms. Moore. And you might take some measures to ensure your tongue doesn't fall out of that open mouth."

"Yes, Ms. Moore." Rachel closed her mouth. "So, how did Indigo's group survive?"

Ms. Moore stopped laughing. "I don't really know how they survived. Indigo told me they struggled for many years. According to the stories he heard, they almost *didn't* survive, many times. But somehow they persevered. And now it appears they need our help. Malgam needs our help."

"Who's Malgam?" Rachel didn't think she had heard that name before.

Ms. Moore considered her. "Did your Pathik say what his father's name was?"

"No." Rachel thought back to be sure she was right. "No, he only ever mentioned Indigo's name."

"But he did say that Indigo was his grandfather?"

"Yes, he did." Rachel suddenly understood. "Malgam was the baby—the baby you and Indigo had."

"That's right, Rachel. He would be Pathik's father. Who is, from what Pathik says, very ill." Ms. Moore's voice was strange; weak and tremulous.

"We'll help them, Ms. Moore."

"But we can't really help them, can we?" Vivian looked confused. "We can't get the medicine across the Line."

"You're right," said Ms. Moore, tears finally slipping down her cheeks. "The worst of it is that I once had a way for us to do just that."

"What do you mean, you had a way?" Vivian's voice was sharp.

"A key." Ms. Moore began to say more, but Vivian interrupted her.

"A *key*? What kind of a key? Where did you get it?"

Ms. Moore was silent. She looked at Vivian for a long time. Vivian stared back. Rachel wasn't sure what was happening. When Ms. Moore spoke again, her voice was almost as sharp as Vivian's had been.

"Do you know something about keys, Vivian? Because if we can help these people, we *must* do it."

Vivian looked away. "I'm sure the boy ran off," she said. "We probably scared him."

"He didn't run off." Ms. Moore leaned toward Vivian.

"He made a long and difficult journey to get here. And he needs our help."

Vivian said nothing. Ms. Moore waited.

Finally, Vivian looked back at Ms. Moore. "I'm sure Rachel is tired," she said.

"What? I am *not* tired."

"It's the middle of the night—of course you're tired." Vivian was using her strict voice. "I'd like to speak with Ms. Moore for a bit, and I want you to rest here while we talk. You can stretch out on the sofa."

"But Mom," Rachel said. "I am *not* tired."

"We can go to the dining room," said Ms. Moore, rising from her chair.

"But *Mom*." Rachel knew it wasn't going to do any good. Once Vivian used the strict voice, there was never any room for negotiation. All she could do was watch Vivian and Ms. Moore cross the hall to the dining room.

CHAPTER 17

Rachel woke with a start. She hadn't meant to fall asleep, but the sofa was surprisingly comfortable despite how firm the cushions were. Somebody had put a blanket over her. She sat up and rubbed her eyes. Her mom and Ms. Moore were whispering, huddled together at the dining room table. Rachel could see them through the doorway from the parlor, where they had told her to stay and rest. She couldn't hear them though. Probably they were busy figuring out how to pretend the whole situation never happened. How to avoid trouble.

Every time Rachel looked at the digim of Indigo, she saw Pathik's face. She wondered where he was right now. She wondered if he was okay. It wasn't winter yet, but the nights were getting pretty cold. She hoped he knew she hadn't deserted him. Most of all, she hoped Ms. Moore meant what she had said about helping him. And that Vivian wouldn't be able to talk her out of it.

Her mom was scared. Rachel could tell by the look on her face—the same look she had that day in Bensen. She'd had that look on her face to some degree or other for as long as Rachel could remember. Worrying about getting Identified, worrying that the government might find them. Rachel had her doubts about that. After all, even if her parents were involved in the rebellion, her dad was dead now. Why would the government waste time looking for her mom? It wasn't like she had any way to cause them problems. They had lived quietly for as long as Rachel could remember without anyone nosing around. If the government was really looking for them, they would have found them by now.

She peered across the hall into the dining room. The two women were still whispering. Ms. Moore looked tired and worried. Vivian had a hand on her shoulder, making little circles like she did when Rachel had a stomachache. Rachel thought it was the first time she had ever seen anyone touch Ms. Moore other than a doctor. She knew she had never seen her get a hug, or more than a handshake from anyone that she could remember. Ms. Moore wasn't the huggy type. The fact that she was letting Vivian comfort her made Rachel think her defenses must be down. She bet her mom was telling Ms. Moore how they should mind their own business and everything would be fine.

Rachel puffed air into her cheeks, making them inflate like twin balloons, then blew out hard, making a noise her mom would have called rude. Neither her mom nor Ms. Moore looked her way. She couldn't stand this anymore. It felt like the digim on the mantel was staring at her; those blue eyes that looked so much like Pathik's. He was out there somewhere, she knew he was, probably cold and scared, but still there. Her mom had said that he probably ran away after he saw her and Ms. Moore tonight, but she knew he hadn't. Pathik wasn't going to run away without doing everything he could to make sure his father was okay.

If *her* dad were there Rachel knew that he would be helping Pathik, not sitting in some room convincing himself why it would be better not to do anything at all. She knew her mom was scared, but that was no excuse for deserting Pathik. She couldn't believe Vivian was actually that kind of a person.

She took several deep breaths, as though she were getting ready to dive under water. She was going to walk right in there and tell her mom what she thought of her, what her *dad* would think of her if he were alive. Vivian might not like hearing it, but it was the truth. Rachel was tired of all the lies. She hopped up off the sofa and started toward the parlor quickly; she didn't want to give herself a chance to change her mind.

"Mom, we have to help Pathik." The two women hadn't seen her approaching, and both turned in surprise.

"We can't just do nothing. He came all this way, and if Dad were here, he would help, and I can't help it if you're scared. You are doing the wrong thing! You're being a coward!"

"Rachel!" Ms. Moore put her hand on Rachel's arm. "You will *not* speak that way to your mother."

"It's all right." Vivian gestured to the empty chair next to her. "Rachel honey, have a seat. You can't really blame her," Vivian said to Ms. Moore. "I haven't been exactly forthcoming with her."

Rachel sat down. She was still buzzing a bit from having actually *yelled* at her mom, but she was also wondering what was going on. Forthcoming? About what? What else could there be besides *your dad and I were collaborators*?

"Rachel, we *are* going to help. Or at least try." Vivian covered Rachel's hand with her own. "And you're right, your dad would have never hesitated. But listen, I'm going to try harder to be brave. Like you." She smiled at Rachel.

"Mom." Rachel felt instantly horrible.

"It's okay, Rachel."

The three of them sat there for a minute, each thinking their own thoughts.

"Ms. Moore, I thought you said you didn't have the key anymore?" Rachel didn't give her time to answer. "What *is* the key, anyway? How does one work? Can we make a new one? Would it work to—"

"Slow down, child." Ms. Moore waved her hand in front of her face as though she were wafting away smoke. "Don't overheat. A key is just what it sounds like. A way to unlock the Line, disable it, at least for a short time. Although it's really a key*card*—like the one your mother uses for the utility vehicle. And mine is still . . . lost."

"Where did you get it? Can we go there and get another one?" Rachel tried to speak calmly, but she found it difficult. Pathik was waiting.

"Indigo gave it to me. I was . . . I was going to Cross with him, as soon as I could. We planned to Cross together, but my parents both got ill. I had to care for them. Once Malgam was born, I was afraid for his safety. I told Indigo to Cross without me, take the baby. I told him I would join him when I could. But then . . . my key was lost."

Rachel was astounded. Ms. Moore had been planning to Cross? That was crazy. It wasn't something she could even imagine. She was trying hard to do just that when she realized what Ms. Moore had just said.

"How did Indigo Cross?"

"What do you mean, Rachel?" Ms. Moore looked puzzled.

"You said Indigo Crossed with the baby. But you still had the key."

"Oh. He had more than one. The group he Crossed with had several, in case something went wrong. Each key only works one time. When Indigo gave me mine, before he Crossed with Malgam, he told me to be very careful with it for just that reason." Ms. Moore bowed her head. "I thought I *was* careful."

"So we have no key, and there's no other way to disable the Line and get the medicine to Pathik." Rachel sighed.

"There may be another key." Vivian squeezed Rachel's hand. "Your father and I knew a man, a long time ago. Peter Hill. He was a collaborator. He mentioned a key one night, when we were having dinner with him and his wife. It's not something he would have said lightly."

"Do you know where he is? Can we contact him?" Rachel felt her heart speed up.

"I think Peter may still be living in Bensen. That's where he lived when I knew him. That's one of the reasons I've always warned you to stay near me when we go there." Vivian's voice broke. "I've just wanted to keep you safe, Rachel. I hope you can understand."

Rachel squeezed her mom's hand back. "I do, Mom. I do understand."

Vivian nodded and swallowed hard. When she continued, her voice was clear. "I'm going to check tomorrow in the streamer's general directory listings. I've never checked before because I've always been afraid of traces, but this is worth the risk. If Peter is still in Bensen, I'll go there tomorrow. I'll ask for his help. He was a good man when your father and I knew him. I think he would help us if he could, even though . . ."

Rachel waited. Her mom didn't say anything more.

"Even though what?" Rachel was almost afraid to ask the question.

"Rachel." Vivian hesitated. "In Bensen . . . the woman and the little girl who were Identified." She grimaced, as if uttering her next words was going to physically hurt. "That woman's name was Jolie. She's Peter's wife. I think the little girl was their daughter." She finished in a rush. "I'm not going to tell Peter we saw Jolie. I need to find out what happened, how much trouble they're in. We have to be careful, as careful as we can be. There was nothing we could have done that day anyway."

Rachel wasn't sure what to say. Her mom had *known* that woman, had known her and *still* walked away when she was in trouble. Yet even though she thought walking away was wrong, Rachel knew the EOs would have just added them to the tally of Identifications that day if they'd tried to help. It would be impossible to make a difference in some jail.

"Mom," she said.

"I know, Rachel." Vivian bowed her head. "You think I'm a coward."

"No, Mom. I was going to say . . . that must have been so hard for you. I'm so sorry that you had to make a decision like that."

Vivian looked up, her eyes glittering.

"Well." Ms. Moore stood up. "It's very late. We need to get some sleep." She stifled a yawn behind her hands. "Tomorrow I will send Jonathan on some sort of errand in the morning, to be certain that he won't be in our way while we work on this. I have some items I'd like to send along with the medicine. I'll need your help gathering them, Rachel, tomorrow, while your mom is in town. For now, let's get some rest."

AFTER THE QUILLENS left, Elizabeth went to the parlor and eased herself down onto the sofa. Her leg hurt. That little jaunt out to the Line had taken its toll. The whole night had taken its toll. She needed a few minutes before trying to climb the stairs to bed. She wondered if Vivian would be able to get a key. It didn't sound likely. Who knew if the man Peter ever even possessed one? Who knew, if he had, whether he still did. Or whether he would be willing to give it to Vivian. Elizabeth wished her own key had never been lost.

Lost. More like *stolen*. Elizabeth still wondered who could have known about it. It could only have been one of the maids, and whoever it was must have taken the key without realizing its true value. They had probably thought it was a cred card—they looked quite similar.

She had put the key in her desk, the desk her father had presented to her on her eighteenth birthday. He had been so proud of being able to afford that desk, handmade by a craftsman in Ganivar. She was thrilled when she saw it, especially entranced by the secret compartment concealed beneath the middle drawer. By that time she had something to hide.

Later, during the months of her mother's illness, and then her father's—those long months when hopeless duty trapped her, kept her away from Indigo and their child—she would go to the desk sometimes when she knew she wasn't being watched and work the series of secret latches that revealed the hiding place. She would take out the keycard to look at it. Just to reassure herself that it was still there, that she still had choices. That Indigo and she could be together someday. The day after her father died, Elizabeth went to the desk and found nothing. The compartment was empty.

She would never forget that moment. She remembered the dry, scratching sound her hands made scrabbling through the desk's empty recesses, like a starving bird trapped in some barren attic. She didn't recall how long she sat there in front of that desk. When she realized the key was gone—not fallen to the drawer below, not on the floor beneath—but truly gone, she began to cry.

Elizabeth didn't want to remember any more about that day, or those tears. She had to be up early in the morning to catch Jonathan in time for him to make the Maglev connection in Bensen. She struggled to her feet, amazed at how much old bones could ache. Time to conquer the stairs.

CHAPTER 18

JONATHAN WAS TINKERING with the misting timer when he heard Ms. Moore say his name. "Early even for you, isn't it?" he said, though he wasn't that surprised to see her. He'd expected something this morning; he just didn't know what. The lights in the main house had been blazing far later last night than they did normally. He'd been keeping a closer eye on the place since the incident in town; making sure his evening walk took him past the house, dropping by to pick up something in the greenhouse after hours. Snooping, if he were to be honest.

He turned around to face her, a gnarled hand shielding his eyes from the glare of the rising sun coming in through the greenhouse door.

For a moment all he could see was her silhouette, her hair lit from behind so it glowed, wisps floating away from her head like they used to forty years before. He wondered fleetingly if her face would somehow look the way it looked so many years ago. Young and pretty. Happy. But when she came farther inside the greenhouse and the shadows revealed her features, they were the same as they had been for too long. Tight. Worried. Closed.

"Yes," Ms. Moore answered. "I suppose I haven't been here quite this early for a long time. I've become spoiled in my old age, too used to dawdling over my breakfast."

"Old age? Well, if you're old, then that makes me something I'd rather not think about. I guess we're all starting to wear out some though." Jonathan pointed to the pieces of a misting timer on the work table in front of him. "Don't know if I can fix that this time. Bushings are gone, and they don't stock them anymore, least not where I can find them in Bensen."

"That is a problem." Ms. Moore picked up the casing of the timer, tracing the empty interior with her finger. "We can't very well manually control all the misting. There's too much of it to be done, even with Rachel's help." She looked at Jonathan. "Do you think Tolliver's might stock the bushings?"

"Tolliver's would have them." Jonathan tilted his hat back off his forehead. "That's all the way to Ganivar though, and you know they won't deliver something that small out here."

Ms. Moore placed the timer casing back on the table. "I was thinking," she said lightly, "perhaps you could drive into town, take the Maglev to Ganivar. You would have to stay over, catch the evening run tomorrow night back to Bensen. I know it's a bit of a trip, but surely there are other items we need that would make it worth it. We could finally get some more hoses." She wandered over to a tray of seedlings. "I wouldn't want to lose Rachel's new cross. They look quite promising, don't you think?" She peered at the tiny green plants in the tray.

Jonathan adjusted his hat again, sliding it forward so his eyes were partially concealed. Then he leaned against the work table and crossed his arms. "You wanted that done today?" he asked, staring at his boots.

"I think today would be fine." Ms. Moore carefully brushed some potting medium off a seedling's tiny leaves. "Unless, of course, you have plans."

Jonathan said nothing. He appeared to be fascinated by the dust coating the toes of his boots. Ms. Moore straightened a seedling in the tray, tamping the potting mix firmly around its delicate roots. "Well, I'd better get Ms. Quillen's day lined out," she said, turning to go.

"Ms. Moore." Jonathan spoke quietly. "I don't know that today would be the time to make such a trip." He didn't look up from his boots.

Ms. Moore turned. "Why not, Jonathan?" she asked, her pronunciation of each word precise. "Did you have some other plans?"

Jonathan shook his head. "Seems to me there has been a bit too much commotion around here lately." He looked up at her. "I just think it might be better if I was nearby, in case we have any trouble."

"What sort of commotion are you referring to, Jonathan?"

Ms. Moore's tone had turned from precise to icy. "What sort of trouble could we have . . ." She paused to ensure her next words were understood. ". . . that would concern *you*?"

Something flashed in Jonathan's eyes, just for a moment. His jaw tensed. But when he spoke, it was in his normal, rather deferential manner. "I've noticed some unusual activity, Ms. Moore, around the place. After dark."

Ms. Moore became very still. She stared at Jonathan for a long time, as though she were looking at a painting in some museum, wondering what the artist could have possibly meant. "Jonathan," she finally said, "what were you doing here at night? Your *work* here is over long before nightfall."

Jonathan nodded, as if a long-anticipated insult had finally been uttered. "I came back for the timer, to see if I had something at my place that might fit." He looked away. "I didn't expect to be interrupting anything."

"I'm not certain to what you might be referring, Jonathan." Ms. Moore took two steps toward him as she spoke— slow, deliberate steps. "However, I can assure you that whatever your concerns are, they are unfounded." She tilted her head slightly, waiting for him to look at her again. She didn't continue until she had his full attention. "Do you think, Jonathan, that we need to have a conversation? Is it necessary to revisit certain topics? Topics on which I *thought* we had reached an understanding?"

Jonathan narrowed his eyes but held her gaze. There was an undercurrent of defiance in his voice when he replied. "Understanding and agreement are not the same thing."

"Good morning." Rachel stood in the greenhouse doorway.

"Good morning, Rachel," said Ms. Moore. "We can get started with repotting in a few minutes. I was just asking Jonathan to go pick up some things we've been needing."

Rachel saw the misting timer in pieces on the work table. "Did it finally break for good, Jonathan?"

"It looks like it did." Jonathan was still staring at Ms. Moore.

"Too bad. Misting is going to be a lot more work without it."

"Ms. Moore is having me make a special trip to Ganivar to get parts, so it will soon be solved." Jonathan picked up the bushings and slipped them into his pocket. "Anything besides these and the hoses?"

"No," said Ms. Moore. "I think that will be all. Let me know if you think you'll be late getting back. I know how unreliable the Maglev schedules can be."

Jonathan didn't reply. He just tipped his hat at Rachel and left.

Rachel and Ms. Moore watched him go.

"Well, that's over," said Ms. Moore.

"Do you think he had any suspicions?" Rachel wasn't certain what she had interrupted, but it seemed like it had been a little tense. She'd never seen Jonathan in such a mood.

"I don't know. I sometimes think I haven't the first idea about what goes through Jonathan's mind." Ms. Moore peeked out the doorway. "He's gone now. And we had better get busy."

CHAPTER 19

WHILE VIVIAN WAS in Bensen meeting with Peter, Rachel stayed at the main house helping Ms. Moore. Her cast had been removed weeks earlier and her leg was almost back to normal, though she still used a cane when she felt tired. Rachel tried to make sure that Ms. Moore didn't do too much. She rummaged through boxes in the cellar until she found the ones Ms. Moore told her they would need and hauled them upstairs to the parlor. She brought kalitea from the kitchen so Ms. Moore could drink it while she poked through the boxes.

"This will probably be useful," Ms. Moore said, taking a small, battery-powered heater from one of the boxes. "And this will be important." She added a square black object to a pile of items.

"What is it?" Rachel asked. She couldn't figure out what most of the things in the pile were, though a few were recognizable. There was the heater. There were thermal blankets made of thin, highly engineered fabric, which could keep a person warm even in a blizzard. She knew about those from watching adventure shows on the streamer. There were tools, some minibeams, and various items of clothing.

"It's a solar charger. A very old one." Ms. Moore picked up the square object. "You open it like this." She flipped a latch, and the square popped open like an old-fashioned book. "You just keep unfolding it until you have an array of panels. Then you can set it up wherever you are to catch the sun. It charges these." She picked up a case from the pile and opened it to reveal ten batteries, each in its own compartment. "They work in all the things here—the heater, the tools, all of it."

Rachel was impressed. "This is all for Pathik, right?"

"This and some other things." Ms. Moore began to pack things in a duffel bag. "Indigo said that they were able to cobble together certain conveniences, but not much survived the initial blasts. I would imagine that most of what did survive wasn't useful once the infrastructure was destroyed." She saw Rachel's puzzled expression. "Power, working plumbing, all those things we take for granted here. Did Pathik say much about the state of things?"

"We didn't have time to say much."

"I see." Ms. Moore pointed to another box. "Could you hand me the folder on top there?"

"What's this?" Rachel lifted a folder full of printouts from the box. A small blue book, bound with real cloth, fell from the folder.

Ms. Moore finished fitting the tool kit snugly into the duffel bag, wedging it next to the heater so that it was secure. She tugged at the drawstrings of the bag, testing them for weakness. "That," she said, "is my own little research project, all about the Line. And that"—she nodded toward the little book—"is my great-grandfather's diary. He was still living when they activated the National Border Defense System. He was a military man. Quite important, from what I understand. And his diary has some interesting tidbits from that time."

Rachel wondered what the printouts said. "I still don't understand how they got away with cutting off all those people. Didn't anybody care? I mean, that was before they even had EOs. It seems like the people could have done something to stop it."

"Well, the people didn't really know *what* was happening, until after it had already happened. There were no public announcements, no warnings given to those who found themselves on the wrong side of the Line. The U.S. government claimed later that if they had attempted to warn people, any communication would have been intercepted by the Korusalian forces." Ms. Moore shook her head. "My grandfather told me some of the stories. I shudder to think of what they went through. Imagine the father who got up that morning, the morning they activated the System, packed his overnight bag, and started the trip back home to Toron from his business trip in Ganivar."

"Toron?" Rachel didn't know where that was.

"Toron used to be a city in the U.S. Now it's a part of Away." Ms. Moore reached for the folder Rachel still held.

"Here," she said, showing Rachel a printout of a map. It looked familiar to Rachel; she recognized it from geography lessons. It showed the U.S., Unifolle, and parts of some surrounding countries. There was a heavy blue line indicating the U.S. System. At the northwest corner of the U.S., the System jagged inland at a sharp angle, cutting across to the Unifolle border. That jag was the Line, though it wasn't labeled as such. The land area to the north of the Line wasn't labeled either, but Rachel knew it was Away.

"See?" Ms. Moore pointed to a spot in the area that was Away. "Toron used to be here. It would have been a short jaunt to Ganivar for a business trip."

Rachel stared at the point on the map, trying to imagine a whole city that no longer existed.

"Think of that father," said Ms. Moore, "trying to return home to Toron from his business trip. As far as he knows, all is well. But halfway home, there is a roadblock. The father is informed by a soldier that he cannot pass. His wife and daughter are waiting at home, the man says, but the soldier tells him no. He is given a number and told to report to a temporary shelter.

"That afternoon, when the father realizes, more swiftly than most I imagine, what has happened, he walks out of the shelter and slips past the sentries. He has decided he will walk all the way to Toron if he has to and fetch his wife and daughter to safety. He walks and walks, and then . . . the stories all ended the same way."

"How?" Rachel was so caught up in the story that she whispered her question.

"He bounces." Ms. Moore was gazing at the map in her hands, but Rachel didn't think she was actually seeing it.

"Against the Line."

Ms. Moore nodded. "You and I *know* what the Line is, Rachel—it's been a part of our experience forever. But to that man, it must have been terrifying. He bounced against thin air, in the middle of a field he must have passed countless times on his trips home. Imagine what he experienced. Think of it. He walks into *nothing*, and is thrown backward. Before he has time to get up, there are soldiers surrounding him, but he manages to get past them once, perhaps twice. He throws himself against—the thing—whatever it is, trying different spots, trying to leap over it. By this time the soldiers have backed off, standing at ready with their guns, letting him wear himself out. Once he has, they carry him, sobbing, back to the shelter. He never sees his wife or his child again." She blinked and looked at Rachel as though she had just realized there was someone else in the room. "They probably died in the blast. There were many, many stories like that."

The two of them sat in silence for a few minutes.

"If I were that man, I would have protested," Rachel said. "I would have done something! Why didn't they do something once they knew?"

Ms. Moore smiled, a small, sad smile. "Oh, but they did, Rachel. At least they tried. Of course, when the System was first activated, in the few days before the Korusalians attacked, people were in shock. And the government issued statements about national security requirements and temporary sacrifices, assurances that the people trapped in the unprotected zones would be fine. But those who had someone on the other side of the Line weren't mollified. Especially when the news broke that certain people, people of wealth or power, *had* been warned prior to the activation of the Line, so that they could gather their families together in safety. They charged the reporter that uncovered that information with treason and executed him."

"Michaels," said Rachel. "Wasn't that his name?"

"Correct." Ms. Moore looked impressed. "Your mom really is quite thorough with your lessons. Though I doubt she is able to get materials that go into much factual detail. There is only the official story anymore."

Rachel nodded. "My mom always tells me the official story isn't necessarily the true story."

"She's right." Ms. Moore shuffled through some of the printouts in the folder. "There are reports in here . . . ah!" She pulled a few pages out and handed them to Rachel. "Reports from various military branches about the events right after they activated the System. All from my great-grandfather's things. There are details in those that were never released to the public."

"Like what?" Rachel flipped through the pages, but they were all in tiny, faded print. She wondered if she could keep them and read them later.

"Yes, it is rather dense stuff, isn't it?" Ms. Moore reached for the papers, which Rachel reluctantly gave to her.

"I remember the high points from reading these so many times." Ms. Moore carefully replaced the pages in the folder. "When they activated the System, riots broke out; mobs charged the border. After the Michaels execution, they declared a police state in the Unified States. People were jailed, and worse. That's when the U.S. government commissioned the EOs and started giving them the sort of power they have now. Power to simply haul people off if they want, with no formal charge."

"Is there stuff in there about Away?"

"There is some." Ms. Moore sorted through more pages, but she didn't take any out. "According to these reports, they were still in contact with the people on the other side of the Line immediately after the attack, through multiple frequency comms. But soon communications became less frequent; the hysterical calls for help died down, and there began to be fewer reports. The ones that did trickle in carried word of strange burns, of people dying after drinking water, of terrible chaos. Within days there was no answer to the comms the military put through."

"Why didn't they disarm the Line and go see what had happened?"

"The U.S. determined that radiation levels were unsafe outside the border and that no rescue efforts could be attempted. They issued a statement saying that as soon as scientists indicated that it was safe to proceed, they would begin relief efforts. Unifolle confirmed their findings. They claimed the U.S. had not informed them that people would be abandoned outside the System and promised they would begin their own emergency rescue efforts as soon as it was safe.

"Days passed, then weeks. All communication from the other side ceased, though they were sent multiple frequency comms every hour. The radiation levels decreased, but other contaminants were detected that the scientists could not identify. No one Crossed the Line. The people abandoned on the other side were left to suffer unknown horrors. The government did keep sending comms, but there was no answer."

Rachel felt like crying. She kept imagining the wife of the businessman Ms. Moore had described. The wife and her little girl, left there, alone and scared. Images of Jolie and her little girl being Identified in Bensen, of the girl screaming and crying, mingled in her mind with those of the faceless woman and child left Away.

Ms. Moore picked the little clothbound book up off the floor where it had fallen. It was blue, with no marking on the cover. The edges were worn and soiled.

"This is my great-grandfather's personal diary." There was a marker in the book, and she opened it to that page. "The government heard only once more from Away, about two months after the bomb was dropped. But they never made public what it was they heard. My great-grandfather copied it word for word in here. I think it frightened him."

She handed the book to Rachel. The marked entry was handwritten in a bold scrawl.

CARSON REPORTS THEY HAVE
CONTACT. A FAINT SIGNAL,
TOOK THEM SOME TIME TO
DECIPHER IT. IT WAS SENT IN
RESPONSE TO THE 2200 COMM
FROM THREE DAYS AGO. THE
STANDARD MESSAGE, "AID TO
ARRIVE AS SOON AS SAFETY
ALLOWS, REPORT ALL DAMAGES,
NEED CASUALTY ESTIMATES,
SITUATION OVERVIEW. PLEASE
RESPOND." THEY SEND THEM
EVERY HOUR. CARSON WAS
SHAKY, NEVER SAW THE MAN
RATTLED BEFORE. THE MESSAGE
THEY GOT BACK READ AS
FOLLOWS:

STAY OUT. WE NO LONGER
REQUIRE YOUR ASSISTANCE.

Rachel looked up with wide eyes. "The Others told the government to stay out?"

"Yes." Ms. Moore reached for the diary. "Can you blame them?"

Rachel thought about how they must have felt when they realized what had been done to them, when they understood that their government had deserted them, discarded them. She thought of Pathik's anger when he had said "We have no doctors."

"No," she said. "I can't blame them at all."

Rachel and Ms. Moore spent a few more hours going through boxes, finding things that might be useful to Pathik and the rest of the Others. Finally, Ms. Moore closed the last box and sat back on the sofa.

"Shall we take a break? We could have another cup of kalitea before your mother returns. The rest of the things I want to send won't be here until tomorrow anyway."

Ms. Moore had made a call to Dr. Beller earlier. Rachel had heard only one side of the conversation, but it was enough for her to deduce that Dr. Beller would be coming to The Property the next day to deliver quite a large assortment of drugs and medical supplies.

Rachel poured fresh kalitea for both of them.

"Does Dr. Beller know about Pathik?" Rachel wasn't sure how much Ms. Moore had told him.

"Dr. Beller?" Ms. Moore frowned, uncertain why his name had come up. Then understanding flooded her face. "Ah, you were eavesdropping during my call this morning." She waved away Rachel's protest. "It's all right. It's as much your business as anybody's." She added some sugar to her kalitea. "Dr. Beller doesn't know anything, except that he will receive double the creds his supplies are worth if he brings them tomorrow. I suppose even at that I should be grateful. He is taking a risk given how closely medical supplies are monitored, though he'll cover his tracks by reporting them stolen."

"Do you think Peter will take the same kind of risk?" Rachel was almost afraid to ask the question, but she had been worrying all day about it. She had realized halfway through the morning that if her mother's old friend had changed, he could easily turn her over to the authorities. What if her mother never returned from Bensen?

"I don't know, Rachel." Ms. Moore considered the question. "Your mother trusted him once. All we can hope is that he is still worthy of that trust." She reached over and touched Rachel's hand. "She'll be back soon. Try not to worry."

CHAPTER 20

H E'S GOING TO do it." Vivian shut the front door of the main house and shrugged off her overcoat.

Rachel hugged her mom. "I'm so glad you're back safe. I was so worried!"

"Oh, honey." Vivian held Rachel tight. "I'm fine. Everything's going to be okay." She released Rachel but gathered her up again right away for another hug and a kiss on the forehead. "Let's go and tell Ms. Moore."

"She's in the parlor sitting down. Her leg is bothering her a little." Rachel followed her mom to the next room. Ms. Moore was sitting sideways, her leg up on the sofa. She smiled as they entered the room.

"Elizabeth, have you taken anything for the pain?" Vivian looked alarmed to see Ms. Moore in such an unladylike position.

"I already offered to get her something, but she refused," said Rachel.

"Oh, it's nothing, just aching a bit. Tell us what happened."

"He was still in the same house. It felt strange going up those steps after so many years." Vivian settled herself next to Ms. Moore on the sofa, careful to avoid bumping her outstretched leg.

"Did he have a key?" asked Rachel.

"He said he can get one. He said he'll bring it here tomorrow night."

"Here!" Ms. Moore frowned.

"I know," said Vivian. "I was worried about that too, but he insisted that the risk of coming to his house twice was too much. He *is* still a collaborator, and they might be watching. One strange visitor might not be noticed, but he was worried that two visits might attract attention. He said he would watch to be certain nobody was following him."

"Well, I guess there really isn't a choice, is there?" Ms. Moore still didn't look happy.

"I really didn't think I could argue too much. It seemed like he was probably right."

"What was he like?" Ms. Moore eased her leg off the sofa, rubbing it.

"Older," Vivian replied. "So much older than I remembered. He looked so tired. Jolie's Identification must be taking its toll."

"I'm certain it must be," said Ms. Moore. "But what I meant was, did he seem suspicious in any way? Did anything make you feel uncomfortable?"

"What do you mean?" Rachel was so happy to hear the news about the key that she hadn't thought past the idea that they might actually be able to help Pathik.

"Rachel, we don't really know what we're dealing with here. Peter was a friend, but your mother hasn't seen him in years. We need to be cautious. You would be surprised at what people you thought were your friends might be capable of doing."

Vivian looked uncertain. "I don't know. I didn't get any sense that he was duplicitous. He was definitely surprised to see me, but once he got over the shock of it, he seemed fine. Really, he treated me better than I deserved to be treated."

Rachel turned to her mother in surprise. "Why would he treat you badly?"

"Because *I* treated *him* badly." Vivian looked at her hands. "Right after your father . . . right after we lost your father, Rachel, Peter came to our house in Ganivar. He came to express his sorrow and to see if there was anything he could do for us. He took a considerable risk to do that. Remember, he was a collaborator too, and the house could have been under surveillance."

"What did you do to him?" Rachel couldn't imagine her mom doing anything *mean* to someone.

"I wouldn't let him in the house. I stood there on the doorstep, staring at him like he was some bothersome salesman. When he was done talking, I told him he needed to leave. I told him to go and not come back, ever." Vivian looked up at Rachel. "Oh, Rachel, you should have seen his face. It closed up just like a fist. But I could see in his eyes he was hurt. He and Daniel . . . he and your dad were great friends."

Rachel went to her mom and knelt beside her. She gave her a hug. She didn't say anything; she really didn't know what to say. She kept thinking about what Ms. Moore had said a few minutes ago. *You would be surprised at what people you thought were your friends might be capable of doing.*

RACHEL CLOSED THE door to the bedroom softly. Vivian had been sleeping for almost twelve hours. The day before, after telling Rachel and Ms. Moore about her meeting with Peter, she had crawled into bed. This morning she had not awakened to go to the main house for work. When Rachel went to check with Ms. Moore that everything was all right, she was told to let Vivian rest as long as she needed. After stopping at the greenhouse to mist her crosses, she tried to fill the hours by tidying the already tidy guesthouse. Ms. Moore had forbidden her to go anywhere near the Line. "All in good time, Rachel," she said. "We need to be ready."

Rachel was worried about Pathik, worried about whether he would come, whether he had even heard Ms. Moore's instructions to return to their meeting place. She was worried about her mother, who seemed so exhausted after going to ask Peter Hill for help. She was proud of her too. She'd had time, while she was waiting for Vivian to return, to think about how hard it must have been for her mother to take the risk.

Rachel peeked in on her once more, then went back to the front room. As she started to sit down, the intercom unit on the wall by the front door beeped. At first, Rachel wasn't sure what she was hearing. The intercom connected to the main house, and it had never been used as far as Rachel could remember. She hurried over to the wall unit. It was a flat panel with two buttons on the top and a round, pin-holed grille below them.

"Hello?" She spoke hesitantly into the grille. The unit beeped again.

"Hello?" A tinny voice came out of the grille. "Vivian? Rachel? If you're there, turn on the speaker."

Rachel pushed the speaker button. "Hello?" she said again, louder this time.

"Rachel?" It was Ms. Moore's voice, sounding a thousand miles away. "Rachel, is your mother awake?"

Rachel was still a bit shocked at the fact that the intercom even worked. "No, Ms. Moore. She's sleeping."

"Wake her," came the reply. "She has a vocall at the main number here. Peter Hill. He said he didn't know how to reach her, so he got the number for The Property. He's waiting. Have her come to the house. And speak up—I can barely hear you."

Rachel leaned down so that her lips were right next to the grille. "Okay!" she shouted, pronouncing each syllable carefully. "I will go and get her now!"

The intercom beeped once more, then was silent. Rachel went to wake her mother.

VIVIAN SAT DOWN in front of the streamer in the parlor to take Peter's call. She looked tired, her hair still mussed after the quick brushing she had given it before hurrying with Rachel to the main house. Rachel hovered near her, worried.

"It's on speaker now, but you can use the earpiece if you prefer." Ms. Moore pointed to a small case on the desk that held accessories for the streamer.

"No. We should all hear what he has to say." Vivian started to push the keypad button to engage the call but hesitated. "Let's not let him know he has listeners," she said. Rachel and Ms. Moore both nodded.

Vivian hit the key to take the call. "Peter?" she said.

"Vivian?" Peter's voice was clear, as though he were sitting in the room with them. "I can't see you."

"The streamer here is an older model, Peter. No video." Vivian waited a moment. "Is something wrong?"

"No, everything is still as planned, Viv. I've got what you need, and I'll be there tonight. I just wanted to check on something." There was a pause. "Are you alone?"

Vivian looked at Ms. Moore. "Yes, I'm alone. What is it, Peter?"

"We didn't have much time yesterday, Viv. I wanted to ask you about . . . well, about certain items. Things Daniel had, Viv. Things he was keeping safe."

Vivian said nothing. Rachel wrinkled her brow and tilted her head at her mother, but managed to keep quiet. Ms. Moore remained impassive, her expression carefully neutral.

"Viv?" Peter's voice broke the silence. "You there?"

"Yes, Peter," said Vivian. "I'm here." She bit her lip. "I think I know what you mean, Peter." She ignored Rachel's pantomimed questions and avoided looking at Ms. Moore altogether. "Is there a reason you're asking, Peter? Do you need those items?"

"No, oh, no, Viv. I just wondered if after Daniel, well . . . if you still had them. It would be good to know they were still safe, just in case they *were* ever needed." Peter lowered his voice so that he was almost whispering. "Do you still have them, Viv?"

Vivian stared at the display on the streamer. "No Video" scrolled across the screen. She had hunched lower and lower in her chair during the conversation, but now she sat up straight. "I do have them, Peter," she said. "Or at least I can get them."

There was a muffled sound from the speaker—an intake of breath, or something that sounded like that—and then Peter's voice again. "That's great, Viv. I figured you would have kept them, knowing how careful you and Daniel were. That's just great." Peter sounded extremely upbeat.

Vivian waited what seemed like a long time before she spoke. "Peter," she finally said, in close to a whisper, "are you sure there's nothing wrong?"

Peter answered quickly. "Nothing, Viv. Although I was thinking it might be wise to relocate them, for safety. If there ever was need, it might be better to be able to get to them quickly. I could take care of that tonight if you like."

Vivian frowned. "We were given very clear instructions though, about not keeping everything in one place. For safety. If you're bringing your item here, it would be better that what I have is *not* here. Isn't that right, Peter?" She waited.

"Yes, of course. As long as you can get them quickly, Viv. In case. Can you do that?"

"Yes."

"Well, I guess if everything is still as we discussed, then I'll see you tonight?"

"Tonight, Peter, as we discussed." Vivian forced herself to smile so that Peter could hear it in her voice. "I'm so looking forward to seeing you. I'll talk to you then." She tapped a key to break the connection.

"Mom . . ." Rachel was silenced by the sight of her mother's face. Vivian was pale, all the color drained from her cheeks. She looked from Rachel to Ms. Moore. "We have a problem," she said. Then she began to shake.

RACHEL WATCHED VIVIAN closely. They had helped her from the desk to the sofa, and Ms. Moore had gone to a cabinet and brought out a decanter filled with some sort of amber liquid. She poured a glass for Vivian and put it in her hand. Vivian couldn't stop shaking for several minutes.

"Peter's planning something." Vivian took a deep breath to try to calm herself. "I know it. He wouldn't have made that call for any other reason. His wife . . . I think he must be planning something in order to help Jolie."

"Is she still in custody, this Jolie?" Ms. Moore's voice was taut, and she looked worried.

"As far as I know. If Jolie is still in custody, Peter will do whatever he has to in order to get her back." Vivian turned to Rachel. "I have something he can use as a bargaining tool, something the government would like to get their hands on. That's what he was asking about. He may be thinking of a trade—what I have for Jolie and his daughter. I'm afraid he won't bring the keycard when he comes. He'll bring Enforcement Officers." Vivian tried to say more, but her voice broke. She covered her face with her hands and began to weep. Rachel knelt next to her mother, trying to comfort her.

"What is it you have?" Ms. Moore sounded annoyed.

Then the front door chimes sounded.

CHAPTER 21

Aꜰᴛᴇʀ ᴍᴀᴋɪɴɢ ᴄᴇʀᴛᴀɪɴ Vivian and Rachel understood they must remain absolutely silent, Elizabeth handed Vivian the stunner and closed the parlor door. She stood in the entryway staring at the front door. She was not expecting any visitors. Dr. Beller had already brought the medical supplies she had requested, leaving with his payment and a puzzled look, hours ago. She'd packed everything into the duffel bag with the other supplies and had Rachel hide it in the greenhouse in preparation for that evening. She listened, but the chimes didn't sound again. Squaring her shoulders resolutely, she walked to the door and squinted through the peephole.

It was Jonathan. Standing on the porch, holding his hat in his hands. Elizabeth thought a moment, then opened the door as far as the safety chain allowed. "Jonathan," she said through the narrow opening. "I take it you didn't go to Ganivar after all."

Jonathan looked uncomfortable. "I need to talk to you," he said.

"I'm sure whatever it is can wait until tomorrow, can't it, Jonathan? I was just getting ready for a bath."

"I don't think it can wait, Ms. Moore."

She eyed him warily, making no move to open the door.

Jonathan waited, turning his hat round and round by its brim. "Elizabeth," he finally said, so softly she almost didn't hear it. She shook her head at him, but at the same time she unhooked the safety latch and motioned him inside the entryway.

"Jonathan, whatever it is, this really isn't a good time."

"I'll try to make this short." Jonathan still spoke softly. He seemed to be having trouble forming his words. "I . . . I've been doing a lot of thinking. About right and wrong. I came to give you something." She saw how tired he looked, lines etched into lines on his old face, a sadness she hadn't noticed yesterday dragging at the corners of his mouth. He fumbled to retrieve something from his coat pocket. "Here," he said simply, holding out a small paper packet, tied with some odd bit of string.

Elizabeth saw how worn it was, dirty from frequent handling, as if someone had often taken it from its resting place and looked at it, then returned it unopened to wherever it was kept. She reached out and took it, hardly believing what she knew to be true.

"I should have never taken it." Jonathan lowered his gaze to the floor. "I didn't want you to go, didn't want to lose you. I thought if I took the card, you'd have to stay, and then we could . . ." He stopped himself. He looked up at her, smiling a crooked smile, eyes shining with tears. "I'm sorry."

Elizabeth looked up from the packet into Jonathan's face. One of her hands rose, as if of its own accord, toward him. It floated there between them for a moment, and even she wasn't certain if she meant to strike him or comfort him with it. She exhaled the breath she had not noticed she was holding in and placed her hand gently on his shoulder. She led Jonathan to the bench in the entryway, helped him sit down. When he had recovered himself sufficiently, the two spoke softly, but urgently, for a few more minutes. Then Jonathan left, taking the packet he had brought with him.

"DID YOU HEAR?" Ms. Moore almost knocked Rachel over with the door as she burst back into the parlor. Rachel had been holding her ear against it, hoping to find out what was going on.

"No!" Rachel lowered her voice. "We *didn't* hear. Who was it? What happened?"

"We have to move." Ms. Moore barked the words like a drill sergeant. "If all goes as planned, the Line will be down in about an hour. We need to get the supplies over the Line now, before Peter shows up. He won't be expecting that, and even if he's sent word to the authorities, I don't think there will be time for them to get out here before we're done."

Rachel and Vivian both stared at her. After a second Rachel found her voice. "The Line will be *down*?"

"Yes." Ms. Moore sounded impatient. "Jonathan is taking care of it. That was him at the door. *He* had my keycard. He'll break into the Crossing Station and use it."

"There are no Crossing Stations here." Rachel was confused.

"The brick bunker, Rachel, at the edge of The Property."

"I thought that was just a maintenance shack."

"Well, you thought wrong. Rachel, we've no time right now for long explanations. Let's go!"

Vivian started moving automatically, but Rachel stayed where she was. Ms. Moore and Vivian were almost out the door before they realized she hadn't stirred. They both cocked their heads at her, asking the same unspoken question. She frowned at them as though she were a teacher confronted with two students who were completely missing the point of the lecture.

"It won't work," she said.

"It's the only chance we have," snapped Ms. Moore. "Now come on!"

"No." Rachel shook her head. "It won't work." She was worried. "Pathik thinks we're coming tonight. He won't know to look for supplies just dumped there. And even if he does look, all that will do is get him caught, if the EOs are really on their way."

Rachel could tell Ms. Moore knew she was right. She

could see it by the way her shoulders slumped. She looked completely defeated. Rachel felt terrible for her at that moment.

Vivian must have seen it too, because she went to Ms. Moore and put a hand on her shoulder. "I'm so sorry," she murmured.

"There is *one* way we can still pull it off," Rachel said. "At least, I *think* it would work."

Vivian turned to look at her. Rachel fixed her mother with a clear gaze, willing her to understand. And after a very long moment, Vivian *did* understand. "No, Rachel!"

"Can you think of any other way? You know there isn't one."

"We don't have to help," Vivian said.

"Then we are just like them. Aren't we, Mom? Just like the people who sent Dad off to die."

"Then *I'll* do it." Vivian crossed her arms.

"And when Peter comes? What do we tell him? He'll have the EOs crawling all over The Property if you're gone. You *can't* do it, Mom. You have to stay here and handle him."

Ms. Moore studied Vivian, then Rachel, clearly confused.

"Do what? Vivian? Rachel?" Ms. Moore's voice was a mixture of desperation and hope. Rachel didn't take her eyes off Vivian. "What would work?"

Rachel was silent. She continued to look at Vivian. She watched her mom's face as it crumpled and felt a strange mingling of love and fear. She'd made her point.

Vivian smiled at Rachel. She could barely get the words out, but she managed. "Rachel will Cross," she said, and then she covered her face with her hands, unable to hold back her tears any longer.

Ms. Moore looked at Rachel. Slowly, she shook her head. "You *can't*, Rachel. The key only works once. We have no way of knowing if the Others still have any keys. If they don't, you wouldn't be able to Cross back."

"I know." Rachel tried to smile at Ms. Moore. She didn't manage it.

"You're right of course. Pathik won't know to look for supplies. But let your mother go, child. Or me. It's my son who needs the medicine. Let *me* go."

"If Mom goes, Peter will know something is up. If you go, who vouches for Mom as her Gainful Employer? How do we explain your disappearance in the first place?" Rachel ticked her reasons off on her fingers. "If I go, you can say I ran away from home—that I was mad about too many chores, or bored all the way out here. Nobody will be suspicious of that."

Ms. Moore was very still. Her eyes were still on Rachel, but she seemed to be seeing something else. She blinked twice, and her focus returned.

"You are a very brave girl, Rachel."

Rachel almost started crying then, but she didn't. She clasped one hand in the other, so tight that the tips of her fingers reddened. "I'm afraid," she whispered. She wanted to be brave. But she wasn't.

"Oh, Rachel." Ms. Moore came to her then and held her. "Don't you see? You can't be brave *without* being afraid. The brave ones are *always* afraid. But they do what they must, even so."

VIVIAN TOLD MS. MOORE they would meet her at the green house. She said she wanted to get some things for Rachel from their place. She rushed around once they were back at the guesthouse, grabbing things, nearly frantic. She found the overnight bag she'd brought with her when they first came to The Property and packed it with all the clothes she could fit. She put the portfolio in it, and some extra digims of herself and Daniel. She got the maps and the copy of the original Bill of Rights from their hiding places and slipped them in, with a hastily scrawled note of explanation. There was no time to think, but Rachel could see she was trying to include everything she thought might help her. Rachel stopped her when she started to stuff in an old, well-loved doll.

"Mom." Rachel put a restraining hand on Vivian's arm. "I don't think I'll need that." She smiled to soften the words.

Vivian had to laugh at herself. "No, you probably won't, will you?" She turned away, put the doll back on the bed, fluffing its dress, arranging its legs so it looked comfortable.

"I could use a hug though." Rachel felt like she was seven years old just then. Vivian turned back to her, put her arms around her. Rachel hugged her as hard as she could, trying to memorize the feeling.

By the time they reached the greenhouse, Ms. Moore was already heading toward the Line, dragging the duffel bag behind her. Rachel relieved her of the bag, and they all made their way to the spot where Pathik had been two nights before. It was broad daylight still, which made them all nervous. The place where Rachel had stood talking to Pathik was obvious; the grass was flat all the way up to the Line.

Vivian pointed to the flattened grass. "We'll fluff this up after . . ." She couldn't continue.

"Well." Ms. Moore sounded breathless. "Here we are. Now we just have to keep testing it."

"Testing?" Rachel felt oddly calm.

"Testing the Line, of course." Ms. Moore put her hand out and pushed at the air. "Still there. When Jonathan fits the key, the resistance will disappear. You'll be able to walk right through. You'll need to go fast, get as far away from here as you can, as quickly as you can. We don't know how long we have until Peter arrives."

"How will she know where to go?" Vivian stood shivering, her arms wrapped around herself.

"I think I know where Pathik may be camped." Ms. Moore poked at the air again. "Indigo told me where he stayed when he was here. It might be the same place. I drew a map for you, Rachel, but I doubt you'll need it. Pathik will be on his way here, after all. Head in that direction." She pointed toward the trees in the distance. "You'll probably meet him halfway." Ms. Moore looked off into Away.

"The map is in the duffel bag. I put some letters in there too. There's one for you. And . . . there are others. I hope you can deliver them for me."

Rachel nodded.

Vivian joined Ms. Moore in staring at the meadow beyond the Line. Rachel kept testing the Line to see if there was still resistance. She wondered if Jonathan actually *was* somewhere now, using Ms. Moore's key to help them. Once again, she couldn't get Ms. Moore's words out of her head. *You would be surprised at what people you thought were your friends might be capable of doing.*

"What's taking so long?" Vivian was worried.

"Should be any time now." Ms. Moore still gazed out at Away.

Rachel gasped. Ms. Moore and Vivian turned to see what was wrong, both of them ready, from the looks on their faces, to panic. Rachel was standing with her arm straight out in front of her, wiggling her fingers in the air. "It's gone," she said, looking amazed.

CHAPTER 22

ELIZABETH TOOK A sip of her kalitea. She had brewed a pot for herself and Vivian as soon as they had returned to the house. Now they sat, waiting, as they had for the past two hours. Dusk had crept up around the old house, peeping in through the dining room windows at them. The only sound was the clink of cups against saucers. When the door chimes finally sounded, Vivian jerked in her chair as though she had been shocked. Elizabeth placed a reassuring hand on her shoulder, then carefully replaced her cup in its saucer and went to the door.

The man standing alone on the porch was not what Elizabeth had expected. Peter Hill was well dressed, his blond hair trimmed in a fashionable style. That didn't surprise Elizabeth, since Vivian had told her he was a Professional. The surprise was his friendly, open face. He looked exhausted, but clear, gray eyes met hers, and when he smiled at her she could see it in those eyes, not just on his mouth.

"You must be Ms. Moore." He extended his hand to her.

"I am." Elizabeth took his hand and led him inside. "I'm glad you've come. Something's happened. Ms. Quillen is this way."

"Peter!" Vivian started to rise from her chair when she saw Elizabeth and Peter in the doorway, but collapsed back into it as Peter crossed the room. Her eyes were red and weary looking. Peter knelt beside her, and she began to cry.

"Oh, Peter," she said. "Rachel's gone. She's gone!" Vivian covered her face with her hands, her body shaking with sobs.

"Viv." Peter gently took her wrists and moved her hands so he could see her face. "Tell me what's happened."

"Look!" Vivian pointed to a piece of paper on the table, a piece of paper on which Rachel had spent considerable time composing a dramatic farewell earlier that day. "She left that. Just the typical teenage angst, but I'm so worried, Peter! She took a pack full of clothes, and we can't find her anywhere. It's getting dark . . ." Vivian fought to control her tears.

The door chimes rang again.

Peter, who had picked up the note to read it, didn't seem to notice. Vivian watched him reading, then looked past him to Elizabeth, who raised her eyebrows imperceptibly.

"I'll just go see who that is," said Elizabeth.

When she had left the room, Peter let the note fall on the table and moved closer to Vivian. He dropped his voice to a whisper. "I need the items we talked about earlier today. Can you get them for me, Viv?"

Vivian pushed him away and scrambled up from her chair. "My daughter is missing, Peter! That's more important to me right now than your maps."

Peter gripped her arm, pulled her toward him. "You had me come all the way out here with the . . . with the item I was given for safekeeping, because you're in some kind of trouble and want to use it for your *personal* benefit, never mind what risk there is to me, to the movement. How can you stand there now and tell me that the fact that Rachel's had a tantrum and decided to run away is more important than the maps? Have you forgotten what's at stake?"

Vivian shook his hand away and glared at him. Peter stared at the red mark he'd left on her arm, breathing hard. When he spoke again his voice was even. "Vivian, I know you're upset, but I promise we will figure this out. Rachel can't be far . . ."

"What do *you* need the maps for anyway, Peter?" Vivian hissed the challenge at Peter's face. For a moment her suspicion and anger almost made her forget her lines, her carefully planned and rehearsed lines. She forced herself to calm down. When she looked back at Peter's face, she was hoping he saw panic and regret in her expression. "Oh, I don't care why you want them. I couldn't give them to you even if I did care. Oh, Peter, I should have been more careful."

Peter waited, uncomprehending. Vivian leaned toward him, her own voice lowered to a whisper now. "Rachel took the pack I hid them in when she ran away. She didn't know. I never told her anything about our work. The maps are with her."

Peter stared at her. He opened his mouth to say something, but no words came.

"Excuse me." Elizabeth stood in the doorway again, this time flanked by two Enforcement Officers. Peter and Vivian stepped apart.

"Officers?" Vivian's voice was shaky. She hoped they didn't notice.

"Are you Vivian Quillen?" The taller of the two EOs brushed roughly past Elizabeth.

"She is Ms. Quillen." Peter moved forward to meet the EO. "I'm Peter Hill. Ms. Quillen's daughter is missing. She's left a note. Probably just a stunt, but we're concerned."

The EO looked at Peter, puzzled. "I'm Senior Officer Gillis." He indicated his badge. "We weren't called on a missing girl. We—"

"I believe there may have been a mistake." Peter spoke quickly, stepping even closer to the EO. "Look here, Ms. Quillen is very upset at the moment. I wouldn't want her more upset because of some official mix-up. Can we just focus on the matter at hand?"

"You said Peter Hill?" The second EO approached, eyes on his digitab. He showed the screen to Gillis. "That name is also noted on the call, sir."

"My name shouldn't be in your call record." Peter looked genuinely confused.

Vivian and Elizabeth stood frozen while Officer Gillis read the digitab screen. Three creases etched his brow as he read the call record.

"I've been all over The Property and no sign of the girl." The voice came from the hallway, startling everyone. Jonathan burst into the parlor. He looked at Ms. Moore, who nodded almost imperceptibly. Jonathan turned to the EOs. "Why aren't you out there looking? Who knows where she's got to by now?"

Officer Gillis looked annoyed. "Look, old man, we weren't called here on a missing girl. We—"

"Why else would anyone call the likes of you?" said Jonathan. "Not like you do much good at anything else out here. Besides eating up taxes. Now go on and put your radar detectors to some use—see if you can't track that girl's genid out there." He looked at the digitab Gillis had taken from his partner. "Is that the gizmo you use to do it? Never actually saw one before."

"Are you saying you called us out?" Officer Gillis cocked his head at Jonathan.

"Are you telling me you don't even know who called you? And you're paid to keep us all safe, aren't you? At least that's what I hear every time I turn on the streamer." Jonathan sounded disgusted. "Look, it's almost dark, and we can't find Ms. Quillen's girl. And as you know, around here is not where you want a young girl lost after dark, brat or not." Jonathan glanced at Vivian. "Beggin' your pardon, Ms. Quillen." He turned back to the EOs. "Now I suggest you crank up your fancy radar and go find her."

Officer Gillis studied the screen before him for what seemed like an eternity. Everyone waited, silent, while he read. Finally, he looked up, first at the other EO and then at Peter. "I guess there's some screwup. But I don't understand . . ."

"Neither do I." Peter sounded frustrated. "We have a missing girl. Now can we please see about locating her?"

"We'll need to run some routine checks here first, verify Ms. Quillen's employment status." Gillis looked at Jonathan and Elizabeth. "Any problem with us verifying the two of you as well?"

"Waste of time," Jonathan harrumphed.

"There's no problem, officer." Elizabeth shot Jonathan a sharp look. "I have a Private Enterprise license on file. Jonathan and Ms. Quillen are Gainfully Employed by me. Go ahead with your verifications. Then go find the child."

THEY DIDN'T FIND her, of course. Rachel was far out of range of any patrol-issue genid detector by the time the EOs scanned the area. They gave up after less than an hour. Officer Gillis assured Vivian that a report would be filed and that Rachel's genid would be added to the list of priority scans. Vivian acted the part of the distraught mother flawlessly. So flawlessly that Elizabeth felt worried for her.

When the EOs drove away, Peter insisted that he would escort Vivian to the guesthouse before he returned to Bensen. Jonathan and Elizabeth protested, saying she should stay at the main house, but Vivian assured them it was fine. She told Elizabeth she would use the intercom to keep in touch in case Rachel showed up. She leaned against Peter as they walked away.

Once she was settled on the couch in the guesthouse, Peter busied himself finding wine and pouring Vivian a glass. He sat down beside her.

"Are you all right?"

Vivian stared dully at him. "She could be anywhere."

Peter hesitated. "I know this is hard, but I have to ask you some questions. I have to know what is going on here. After Daniel . . . after you left Ganivar, I couldn't find you. I came looking for you, Vivan. Did you know that? I looked everywhere I could think of, every *way* I could think that wouldn't risk drawing attention. I . . . had something to tell you. And then out of nowhere, you appear and ask for the key? What is happening, Vivian? Why did you want the key?"

Vivian was ready. She'd memorized the story, so she hardly had to think.

"I just couldn't do it anymore, Peter." Fresh tears slipped down her cheeks, real tears. "After Daniel was lost, I tried. I brought Rachel out here where I thought she would be safe. But the years . . ." She stared at him, eyes bright, unable to speak for a moment. "Oh, Peter," she cried, "they just go on and on."

When she continued she spoke softly, so that Peter had to strain to hear her.

"Rachel is almost grown. I just decided to go . . . to go where he was. That's why I wanted your key. I decided to

Cross. I didn't care anymore what might happen to me. I didn't care about anything." She covered her mouth with her hand, fighting back sobs.

"But as far as you know, he's—"

"I didn't *care* anymore. And now look—Rachel is gone. I've been so selfish; I haven't paid enough attention to what might be bothering her. And now she's lost, just like Daniel."

Peter tried to soothe her, but all he could do was wait for the worst of the tears to subside. When she was calmer, he got her another cup of wine. He said he would go back to Bensen and do some checking there. Before he left, he put his hand on Vivian's shoulder. She did her best not to shrink from his touch.

"Try not to worry," he said. He spoke softly, but his next words were chilling to her.

"We'll find her, Vivian."

CHAPTER 23

RACHEL WASN'T SCARED at first. It was so surreal; it was like she was watching a stream show instead of living it. The idea that the Line was just gone for a moment, that she could walk right into the meadow. The idea that she couldn't walk back out. The way her mom was crying when she hugged her and how Rachel had kept thinking it was the last hug she would get from her. Ms. Moore smiling at her, which was weird all by itself, since she hardly ever did. She had kept pointing off toward the trees, telling Rachel to hurry. And finally Rachel let go of her mom and walked away.

Ms. Moore and her mom stood there at the Line for a long time. Each time Rachel looked back, they were still there. Her mom was waving her arm, getting smaller and smaller. She thought they must have gone back to the house once she reached the trees, but she didn't know. All she knew for certain was that she couldn't see them anymore.

Rachel walked fast, as fast as she could with the two bags. They were so heavy. Part of the time, she had to drag the duffel bag Ms. Moore had packed, but she managed to hitch her mom's bag over her shoulder and carry it that way. She looked around while she walked, trying to take in the fact that she had Crossed. She was *Away*.

She had walked for about an hour before she started getting worried. She tried to keep going in the direction Ms. Moore had told her to, keeping an eye out in case the ground opened up in front of her and some strange sheep-cat creature erupted from the hole. There was no sign of Pathik, and she started wondering if he was even still around. What if he had thought it was too dangerous to stay? What if he had gone home, wherever that was? She could be wandering around lost forever.

She decided to check out the map Ms. Moore said she had packed. She stopped beneath a huge old tree and worked her mom's bag off her shoulders, dropping it to the ground next to the duffel bag. For a minute she stood very still, listening to see if she heard anything suspicious. Keeping an eye on her surroundings, she fumbled with the drawstrings on the duffel bag. The map was right on top. Ms. Moore had used the back of an old printout on orchid culture: *Dendrobium Rest/Growth Requirements*. Seeing it made her think of her special crosses. She would never see their blooms, never know what her experiment had produced. She hoped Ms. Moore would take care of them.

The map was pretty simple. Ms. Moore had drawn a

picture of the greenhouse, with the Line labeled. There was a circle a little farther out, labeled "Oak Trees." There was a long line ending in an arrow drawn out from the oak trees, along which Ms. Moore had written "Follow the setting sun." That was it.

Great. Rachel looked up at the sky, where the sun was indeed setting. She had been walking in about the right direction, at least. But how far was she supposed to go? Would she still be alone out here when the sun did set and the dark rose up around her?

She closed the duffel bag and opened the bag Vivian had packed. There was a bottle of water on top, which made Rachel realize how thirsty she was. She opened it and drank, finishing it in two long gulps. She saw the sleeve of her winter jacket peeking out of the bag and pulled it out. The sight of it made her want to cry; autumn wasn't even over yet, but her mom had packed her winter jacket. It made the fact that she wouldn't be home when winter did come seem very real. She put the jacket on, even though it wasn't that cold. That was when she heard Pathik say her name.

CHAPTER 24

AFTER SHE SAW Peter leave, Elizabeth checked on Vivian through the intercom. When she was satisfied that all had gone as planned and that Vivian was steady enough to be alone, she tried to focus on reading for a while before bed, but she couldn't get her mind off of Jonathan. The pain in his eyes when he came to confess, to try to put it right. The pain that was still in those eyes tonight when he left her. He thought he had been responsible, all these years, for taking away her life, the life she could have had. She thought of the ease with which she could have comforted him, had she only told him the truth she was afraid to admit even to herself.

WHEN SHE DISCOVERED she was pregnant, Indigo and Elizabeth had agreed she would go with him Away. They had planned carefully, setting everything in place, trying to think of every possible obstacle. But the day she was to Cross, Elizabeth had found her mother on the floor in the kitchen, feverish to the point of delirium. Her father had called Dr. Beller, but none of the drugs he prescribed touched her illness.

After two months, Dr. Beller wanted them to send her to specialists in Ganivar. The specialists tried various treatments, but nothing helped. Elizabeth's mother died just as new life was stirring within Elizabeth, never knowing she was going to be a grandmother. Elizabeth's father took to his bed soon after. He was so lost without his love, nothing seemed to matter to him anymore. Jonathan had been working on The Property for almost a year by then, and he took over much of the business while Elizabeth looked after her father.

She met Indigo whenever she could, stealing moments between caring for her father. She told him that as soon as her father was back on his feet, they would be together. She dreamed of him at night, thought of him waiting for her in his tiny camp near the pool in the west meadow.

Her pregnancy began to show. She tried to hide it, but soon even the baggiest clothes didn't conceal her growing belly. Jonathan thought she had been raped at first, was ready to hunt down the rogue who hurt her. When Elizabeth told him she had not been attacked, he did everything he could to help her. Through those long months during her father's decline, it was Jonathan who made sure the orchid shipments went out on schedule. If they needed supplies from Bensen, Jonathan made the trip.

He came to find her in the greenhouse when it became clear that her father wouldn't live much longer, to offer her marriage. He told her not to worry about the child coming, that it was a part of her and so he would love it as he did her. When she had to tell him she was in love with someone else, he grew cold. His face seemed to turn to stone right before her eyes.

She had been certain that Jonathan never suspected the father of her child was one of the Others. But after that day in the greenhouse, he began to watch her, to keep track of her comings and goings. His scrutiny made her afraid for Indigo's safety. If Jonathan ever saw Indigo, ever got proof that he was not one of the town boys, he would have immediately alerted the authorities. If they found Indigo, Elizabeth knew they would kill him. By then, fear of the Others was a given in that part of the country—they were the bogeymen in children's bedtime stories. Elizabeth had been afraid too, before she knew Indigo, so she understood that Jonathan would think he was doing the right thing.

Malgam was born three weeks before Elizabeth's father died. It was a difficult birth. Jonathan saved her life that day. He came looking for her when she didn't show up at the greenhouse in the morning, found her in her bedroom screaming into a pillow, and summoned Dr. Beller despite her protests. Elizabeth hadn't wanted the birth attended by any doctor. There was a new procedure—genid recording— at every birth now. The government claimed that recording each person's individual genetic identification would do everything from simplifying record keeping to improving medical response in an emergency, but Elizabeth didn't want her baby's genid recorded. She had no idea what the DNA

analysis would reveal. Thankfully, Dr. Beller was quite ame-
nable to skirting the new genid recording procedure, once he
was given the proper incentive of enough bonus creds.

Elizabeth's father was fading fast, but he seemed to be
aware of Malgam. As soon she was able to, she took the
baby to her father's bedroom to show him. He hadn't said
a word about her pregnancy, even when it was obvious she
was with child. But when he saw Malgam's face peering out
from the blankets Elizabeth had wrapped him in, her father
seemed to become fully lucid for the first time since he'd
taken to his bed. He studied the baby for a long time. Then
he whispered something Elizabeth didn't understand. She
leaned closer to him, asked him to repeat it.

"An interesting cross, I'd say." She could still hear the
smile in his voice.

Indigo stayed near as long as he could, but it was so
dangerous. Elizabeth was afraid every day that he would be
discovered. She knew she couldn't hide Malgam's presence
from prying townsfolk much longer, and she couldn't just
abandon her father. Finally, she told Indigo to take Malgam
and go back to his people. He didn't want to go, but Elizabeth convinced him it was the best thing. She told him that
as soon as she could, she would use the keycard he had given
her and come to him.

UNTIL PATHIK APPEARED Elizabeth had almost succeeded
in not thinking about that anymore. About whether she

would have had the courage to actually take that step—Cross the Line—if her option to do it hadn't disappeared with the keycard. That was the thing she couldn't tell Jonathan earlier, when he had come to right his wrong. That she didn't know, would *never* know, if she would have actually used the keycard after her father died.

Indigo and Malgam had been Away for weeks by then. In those dull days before her father's death, the love that she had found with Indigo, the notion that everything could be different, began to feel like a dream. Even her baby seemed unreal, faded to a translucent image in her mind.

She was not yet nineteen years old. The idea of leaving everything that was familiar to her, of going to a strange place she had been raised to fear, became overwhelming. When, the morning after her father's death, she went to her desk and found the keycard missing, Elizabeth was flooded with so many awful feelings. But the worst feeling, and the one she would never be able to let herself forget, was *relief*.

She knew that was why Indigo never returned for her. He knew things like that. He had always known, in some strange way, exactly what she was feeling, sometimes before she knew herself. He would have come back for her at any cost, she knew it, if only she had wanted him too with her whole heart. But he would have felt her doubt, he would have known how uncertain she was, poor stupid young woman. She knew how much that must have hurt him.

Elizabeth knew she would have to tell Jonathan the truth of it soon; to let him go on bearing the burden he did would be wrong. Tonight though, she had enough to do trying to stay in her seat. For the fears of the past didn't trouble her anymore; she had a son somewhere, a grandson. Indigo— her love—could still be alive. She wondered if he could ever forgive her her cowardice. She might have had a whole new life waiting for her somewhere across that Line if she hadn't been too frightened to Cross so many years ago. She wasn't afraid now. She wanted to stand up and walk outside, leave everything she knew and begin again. It had been all she could do to stay with Vivian while Rachel Crossed.

But the disappearance of an old woman couldn't be explained away by saying she ran off like a teenager. If Elizabeth had Crossed with Rachel, she would have jeopardized Rachel's safety, perhaps Indigo's as well. She could not act. She could only sit and wait, playing absently with the ring on her necklace, and try not to stare too longingly out the window toward Away.

CHAPTER 25

PATHIK CAME THROUGH some underbrush right behind her. She hadn't heard him at all until he spoke. He peered at her as though he were trying to see past some sort of mirage, as though he knew she couldn't be real.

"What are you doing here?"

"Change of plans." Rachel felt oddly shy, now that she was standing right next to him. He was taller than she remembered, and he moved with an ease she hadn't noticed before. She explained as quickly as she could what had happened.

"This Peter," said Pathik. "How do you know he won't just be waiting for you if you do get back?"

"*Can* I get back?"

Pathik studied her and then looked away. "I don't know."

"What about a Crossing Storm? Can't I just wait for one of them and go back that way?"

"A Crossing Storm?" Pathik regarded her with interest. "You know about those?"

"Wouldn't that work? I mean, in case there are no more keys."

Pathik shook his head. "That's not how it happens."

Rachel felt something—hope, perhaps—fade within her. She wanted to ask what Pathik meant, but she wasn't sure she would be able to speak without crying.

"We'd better go." Pathik nodded at the bags on the forest floor behind her. "Can you handle the smaller one?"

"I handled both of them all the way here." Suddenly Rachel felt like hitting him. *Could she handle the smaller one.* Like she was some sort of weakling. It was his fault she was stuck out here, his fault she might never get back home. She walked to the bags and slung her mom's over her shoulder. When she picked up Ms. Moore's duffel bag, Pathik walked over, shaking his head, and took it from her.

"I was just asking a question." He shrugged and then turned and started walking. "It's not too far," he said over his shoulder.

Rachel stood there a moment, narrowing her eyes at his back. Then she hitched the bag higher on her shoulder and followed him.

They walked quickly, so quickly that Rachel had some difficulty keeping up. She didn't say anything. She wasn't about to let *him* know. But she kept falling behind, until finally he noticed. He stopped and waited until she reached him.

"We do have to go pretty fast if we want to get there before dark."

"I thought you said it wasn't far."

"*I* don't think it is. But I'm usually by myself when I make the trip, so it goes a little faster."

Rachel sputtered. She wished she could think of some smart thing to say to him, but her brain seemed to be working at about half speed. She settled for action, and walked past him without a word. She heard him make a derisive sound behind her and whirled around.

"What did you just say?"

"Nothing." Pathik held both hands up as though he were surrendering. "Look, I just want us back at camp before dark."

"Well, let's go then." Rachel was furious. Somewhere inside she was just afraid, but the fury *felt* better. She turned and started walking again.

For a short time they walked in silence. Rachel couldn't see Pathik, but she assumed he was still behind her. Her assumption was confirmed shortly.

"Rachel."

She heard him, but she ignored him.

"Rachel, stop."

Rachel sighed and stopped. She refused to turn around though. She heard Pathik laugh softly.

"Look, we need to make time, but we also need to be somewhat quiet."

She faced him. "I *am* being quiet!"

Pathik held a finger up to his lips. "Seriously. Quiet. You don't really want to attract a lot of attention out here if you can help it."

Rachel didn't like the sound of that. "Are there sheep-cats?" She was whispering now.

Pathik gave her an odd look. He started to reply, but then just shook his head. "Look, follow me, and try to step where I step. We'll be at camp soon, but we need to be careful right now. Kinec and Jab will have a fire going, so we'll be safer then." Pathik moved ahead of her and began to walk again.

"Who are Kinec and Jab?" Rachel tried to focus on placing her feet wherever Pathik had just stepped. She almost fell a couple of times.

"They came with me on the trek."

"Trek?"

Pathik stopped. Rachel ran into him; she had been looking at the ground.

Pathik turned slowly to face her. He was clenching his jaw; Rachel could see the muscle just below his cheekbone jumping. It made her feel strangely triumphant.

"Rachel."

"Yes, Pathik?" Rachel used her sweetest tone.

"Let's just go. As *quietly* as we can. Okay?"

Rachel glared. "After you," she said.

CHAPTER 26

VIVIAN LOCKED THE guesthouse door behind Peter. After answering the intercom buzz to assure Ms. Moore that all was well, she fell onto the couch, exhausted. Peter had said he would be in touch. She dreaded what that might mean, but she was so filled with the emptiness in the room that theories about what sort of trouble Peter might actually represent were beyond her. She wondered where Rachel was right now. Was she with the boy, Pathik? Was she safe with him? Was she warm enough?

She looked around the room at all the things that reminded her of Rachel. The afghan, which Rachel used to snuggle under when she was sick with a cold. The book of short stories they had started reading together—it seemed like months ago—with a slip of paper marking where they had left off. Her shoes—oh! Vivian had forgotten to pack Rachel's newest pair of shoes. She was surprised to feel tears threaten again. She had cried so much today she didn't think there were any tears left.

She couldn't quite believe that Rachel was gone. That she might never tuck a stray tendril behind one of those sweet ears again, never roll her eyes at the latest net book Rachel was reading. It seemed to her that at any moment Rachel would emerge from the bedroom and ask if she wanted to read a story.

She got up and walked over to the bedroom door. The room was in disarray from the frantic packing she had done before Rachel Crossed. The beds were unmade, and clothes that had been rejected as impractical were strewn everywhere.

Vivian crossed to the dresser, drawn by a digim of Rachel. In it, Rachel was holding her newest tray of crosses, smiling at Vivian. Her hair was falling in her eyes, she had a smudge of dirt on her cheek, and she looked absolutely beautiful. Vivian stroked the surface of the digim, her mouth crumpled into a grimace of pain. Rachel. Away.

Just like Daniel, but Vivian tried not to think about that. Daniel was probably dead. Rachel was alive. Vivian had to hold on to that and believe that someday she would see her daughter again. Somehow it would happen. If she could have at that moment, Vivian would have Crossed the Line without hesitation. She would run into that unknown territory without a second thought, run after Rachel, keep running until she held the girl in her arms.

But there was Peter to think of, Peter and the danger he posed to Rachel. If Vivian disappeared, he would put it all together somehow, figure out that she and Rachel had

Crossed. He would get it out of Jonathan, or perhaps even Ms. Moore, though Vivian thought that might be difficult. Peter had a key. He might send people after them, especially if he thought Rachel had the maps. She worried about that—because Rachel *did* have them.

Peter must want the maps to trade for Jolie's freedom. Vivian wished now she hadn't told him that Rachel unknowingly took them when she ran away; at the time she couldn't think of another reason why she wouldn't be able to hand them over when he showed up at The Property. When the EOs had shown up right behind him, she knew she was right to send them with Rachel. It would have been a great trade for him: her and the maps in return for Jolie's freedom. And if she were rotting in some jail, or dead, what about Rachel? What if she managed to Cross back? Who would be waiting?

Besides, Daniel would have protected those maps with his life. Vivian knew she had to do the same thing. Rachel might be able to get them to someone Away who could use them, someone who could make a difference.

Vivian walked back out to the living room and fell upon the couch again. She tugged the afghan out from between the seat cushions and wrapped herself in it. She was so tired, but she knew she wouldn't sleep until her body had absolutely nothing left to fight with.

She reached for the volume of short stories, hoping to find some peace in doing something she had so recently done with Rachel. She flipped the book open to the marker.

There was handwriting on the scrap of paper, and as she removed it from the pages of the book she realized it was a note—from Rachel. She could tell it had been hurriedly written—Rachel's normally neat cursive was a bit scrawled.

> *Dear Mom,*
> *There's not a lot of time—not enough*
> *to say all the things I want to say.*
> *I love you. I know you love me. I'm*
> *not scared.*
> *I know Dad would be proud—of both*
> *of us. Don't worry about me.*
> *Rachel*

Vivian clutched the note to her heart, rocking softly, filled with a simple gratitude at this keepsake—a gift from her daughter, a sign that all was well between them. She wept. Minutes later slumber took her, wrapped in her afghan, holding Rachel's farewell.

CHAPTER 27

WHEN THEY ARRIVED at the camp, Pathik introduced Rachel to Kinec and Jab. Kinec had a friendly look about him, and chubby cheeks that didn't fit with Rachel's idea of surviving in the wilderness. Jab was wiry, with hair as white as sugar. They were both about Pathik's age, though Jab looked younger because he was so small. Neither one was as handsome as Pathik.

Rachel had decided he *was* handsome during their hike to the camp. Though the way he kept telling her to speak more quietly or to look where she was going was annoying. By the time they finally got there, she was beginning to think his looks were his only good attribute.

Kinec smiled and said hello, but Jab just nodded. He kept looking at Rachel like she was to blame for something. She decided to ignore him and followed Pathik to the little campfire. He dropped the duffel bag near it. "You can set up your bedroll here for tonight," he said. "Tomorrow we'll start back to base camp."

Rachel was opening the duffel bag to see what she could use to make a bed when she felt a twinge in her temple. It felt hot and sharp, but it was gone as quickly as it came. She dug around in the bag and found the thermal blankets Ms. Moore had packed, still in their shrink-wrap packages. There were some freeze-dried food packets too. Rachel was trying to remember what else she and Ms. Moore had packed that might be useful, when the pain stabbed at her again, sharper this time. She pressed against her temple with her hand and she must have made a sound, because Pathik was by her side in an instant, asking her what was wrong. Before she could say anything, he turned to Jab.

"Jab!" Pathik sounded angry. The pain in Rachel's head vanished.

"It was only a nudge, Pathik." Jab was standing about fifteen feet away, looking irritated. "I just wanted to see if it worked on Regs."

"Never again, Jab." Pathik's voice was harsh. There was no hint of a smile on his face at that moment. "You know better. Leave her alone." He sounded disgusted. "You and Kinec go get some wood for the fire."

He turned back to Rachel, dismissing the two boys. "Sorry. It won't happen again." He looked worried.

"*What* won't happen again?" Rachel didn't like the look on Pathik's face, or the look on Jab's as he walked away with Kinec.

"We need to talk." Pathik took one of the packaged blankets from her and ripped open a corner of it with his teeth.

"Nice," he said, inspecting the fabric. "This will keep you warmer than anything we have." He unfolded it and laid it down on the ground, removing a rock that would have poked her in the back during the night. "Have a seat." Pathik patted the blanket and settled himself on a corner of it. Rachel sat down next to him, wondering what was on his mind.

"You got a pain, here, right?" He touched his own temple where she had pressed her hand against hers. Rachel nodded. Pathik looked behind him to check on Jab and Kinec. They were picking up sticks, far enough away that they wouldn't overhear the conversation. When he was satisfied they would be busy for a while he turned back to Rachel. "You know that thing?"

Rachel didn't. She shrugged. When Pathik said nothing more, she raised her eyebrows at him. Finally she asked, "*What* thing?"

"That *thing*," he said, as though she should know exactly what he was talking about. "You call it my . . . my sniffing thing." He didn't look happy about having to say that phrase out loud.

"Oh, *that* thing!" Rachel nodded again. "Right."

"Well," he said, "*we* call them gifts. Some of us have them right away, when we're babies. Some of us get them later, when we're little kids. If we get one, we're named for it, either at birth, if it's an obvious gift, or later, if our gift doesn't show right away." He looked at her to see if she understood. "Like Pathik—for empathic, you know." He nodded back toward the other two boys. "Kinec," he said "can make things move."

Rachel must have looked skeptical because Pathik's next words sounded a little defensive. "He *can*," he said. "Not big things, at least not yet. But I've seen him make a pack jump." Pathik got up and started gathering some twigs from the ground. "Jab," he said, without looking at her, "can jab. He can make you hurt somewhere. That's what he did to you just now." He piled the twigs on the fire. The flames ate them greedily.

Rachel didn't say anything. Pathik kept adding twigs and dry leaves to the fire. Maybe all those stories she had read about the Others—all the horrible things they were supposed to have done, things that seemed impossible for a person to do—were true.

Ms. Moore hadn't said anything about weird powers, so maybe she didn't know. Maybe Indigo had only told her part of the truth. Rachel thought about Pathik's sniffing thing. It had seemed harmless when she was still safe on The Property. She hadn't really believed him when he explained it anyway. But Jab—that had *hurt*. And here she was stuck with them, no way home, no way to fight back. She snuck a look at Pathik. He was looking right back at her, smiling a little smile.

"He won't try it again," Pathik said. "He'll be punished for it when we get back to base camp too." His smile disappeared and he looked very solemn. "We have rules about gifts. We're very careful."

"I don't understand." Rachel had so many questions she didn't even know where to start. "*Why* do you *have* gifts?"

Pathik shrugged. "The bomb, I guess. That's what most of the old-timers think. They tell the story still, about the early days. When the bomb went off, it did something to the people who were exposed to the radiation, *changed* something. For the first three years after the blast, the babies all died. Most were born dead; others lived a few days. During the fourth year, two babies lived. More lived each year after that. But as the babies grew, some of them could *do* things. Things like Jab can do, or Kinec. Or me. Things that Regs could never do. And that's how it's been for, well, forever."

"What are Regs?"

Pathik looked embarrassed. "Regs are people like you. People who can't do anything extra."

"What about Indigo?" She had been thinking about what Pathik had said about names, about how the Others named their children for their gifts. Indigo didn't sound like a name that meant anything giftlike. "What's his gift?"

Pathik smiled again. "He says he never developed one. He was named for the color of his eyes, and he has kept that name his whole life."

"Does that make him a Reg?"

Pathik looked indignant. "Of course not. Regs are only, well, only people who come from the other side."

He sat down next to her again, but he didn't look at her. "We *are* grateful to you, Rachel. Grateful for your help. It was brave of you to take the risk." He twisted a twig between his fingers, shredding the bark.

"Are you afraid?" His eyes remained on the twig, and he asked the question so softly she almost couldn't understand his words.

"Should I be?" Rachel looked at his face. She couldn't see anything frightening there, but she was beginning to realize that she knew very little about the Others. Pathik looked up and caught her staring at him. He stared back, his expression unreadable.

"We're not monsters." He reached over and touched the back of her hand with the twig he held, a gentle tap. "No more than Regs are monsters." He tossed the twig away and stood, held out his hand to help her up. "Let's figure out what there is left to eat. We'll need to get to sleep soon so we can start back early in the morning."

That reminded Rachel of the food packets Ms. Moore had packed. She rummaged in the duffel bag and came up with two of them; cheese casserole and meatloaf. She showed them to Pathik, who laughed. "The boys will love those," he said. "A change from dried rabbit." He called to Kinec and Jab, who were heading back with the sticks they had gathered. They did love the food; even Jab seemed to approve of Rachel a bit more after he ate.

They spent most of the rest of the evening redistributing the items in the duffel bag between the three packs Pathik and the others had brought, so that they would each have only one pack on the trip back to base camp. They were all impressed with the thermal blankets. Jab sneered at the tools and the heater, muttering about the useless weight they would add to the packs. Rachel was perplexed by that until Pathik pointed to the batteries.

"They won't be much good once those are used up," he said, almost apologetically.

"Ms. Moore thought of that," Rachel said. She took quite a bit of satisfaction from the look on Jab's face when she pulled out the solar battery charger and explained how it worked.

Rachel kept the overnight bag Vivian had packed close to her. When she was getting her jacket from it earlier, she had seen the portfolio tucked into an inside pocket. She wanted to wait until she had some privacy to see everything her mom had put into the overnight bag. She hadn't been paying close attention when Vivian was packing—she guessed she had been too overwhelmed by the prospect of actually Crossing. She hoped that Vivian had been thinking more clearly than she had.

AFTER THEY FINISHED organizing their packs, it wasn't long until Kinec and Jab wrapped themselves in thermal blankets and got comfortable for the night. Pathik and Rachel stayed up, watching the fire die down to embers and talking in low voices. Rachel had found the letters from Ms. Moore in the duffel bag; one to her, one to Indigo, one to Pathik, and one to Malgam. She tucked hers away in her bag. She gave Pathik the letter Ms. Moore had addressed to him, along with the ones for Indigo and Malgam. "That's

your dad, right?" Rachel pointed to the envelope with Malgam's name on it. Pathik looked surprised.

"I never told you my father's name," he said. "How do
you know it?"

"Ms. Moore knew it." Rachel watched him to see what
his reaction would be. Did he know that Ms. Moore was his
grandmother, or would he learn that when he read her letter?
He didn't say a word, but he did give her an odd look.

"What is your dad's gift?" Rachel asked. "What does it
stand for?"

"He says it means a mixture," said Pathik. "A combination
of elements. It was his birth name. I don't think he has a gift."

"Wouldn't you know by now?"

Pathik shrugged.

"What was your birth name?"

Pathik chuckled. "I'll never tell.

Rachel was tired, but she didn't want to go to sleep yet.
She had never slept outside. There were a lot of noises. She
kept thinking about what the Others' base camp would be
like, wondering what was going to happen when they got
there. She hoped Pathik would stay up with her for at least
a little while longer.

"Do you want to see a digim of *my* dad?" Rachel opened
her bag and found the portfolio. She took out the stack of
digims her mom and she had looked at together so many
times. On top was a picture from a long time ago. It showed
her mom and dad sitting together in their old living room.
It was taken right before she was born, and Vivian's belly

was huge. Vivian laughed every time she saw that digim. Rachel handed it to Pathik.

"That's your mom, right?" Pathik smiled. "She looks nicer here than she did when she was dragging you away the other night."

"She's usually a lot nicer than that. You saw her at a bad moment." Rachel started to tell him that the baby she was carrying in the digim was her, but his gasp silenced her.

"What?" Rachel looked around, trying to see what had alarmed him. "Did you hear something?"

Pathik was pointing at the digim he held. "Why," he whispered, "do you have a picture of Daniel?"

THE FIRE WAS almost out now. It was so dark—the sky was clear, but there was just a sliver of moon. No other light. Pathik was asleep; Rachel could hear him breathing next to her. She didn't think he had believed her when she told him the man in the digim was her dad. He just kept shaking his head, saying, "That's Daniel." He wouldn't tell her how he knew him, or when he had seen him last, no matter how much she begged. Finally, he said she would have to speak to Indigo when they got to base camp. But he *knew* him. That meant that somewhere, somewhere *Away*, her dad was still alive. Or could be.

Four more days of hiking to get to the camp, that's what Pathik said. Four more days and Rachel might find her dad. She stared at the glowing crescent of moon above her, wondering where she would be when it was full again.

THANKS TO:

Richard Baldasty, Dan Butterworth, Beth Cooley,
Meara Nelson Downey, Heidi Gast, Millie Hall,
Janice Joseph, Scott Kramer, Debbie Kyle,
Neesha Meminger, Alexis Nelson, Kelly Pederson,
Mikaela Pederson, Mary Jayne Veljkov, Tom Versteeg.

THEY EACH KNOW WHY.

Kirby Kim and Kirsten Neuhaus.

BEST AGENTS EVER.

Kathy Dawson.

EDITOR EXTRAORDINAIRE.

And thanks to the team at Dial:
Jenny Kelly, Regina Castillo, Lauri Hornik, Claire Evans,
Jen Haller, Jackie Engel, and Deborah Kaplan, as well as
the whole Penguin team.

SO IMPRESSIVE.

The Line *is being used in classrooms nationwide to foster discussions in subjects ranging from Language Arts to Social Studies. Below is a sample of the free, comprehensive classroom guide by Natalie Lorenzi available for use with* The Line. *To download the entire guide, including questions, vocabulary words, and classroom activities, please visit* **www.terihall.com/stuff**.

Discussion Questions for *The Line*

1. Rachel's mother, Vivian, says, "It is always a person's own actions that bring about any real changes, good or bad." Do you agree? Why or why not? Give examples to support your opinion.

2. Before Vivian found her job at The Property, she had been worried that she would end up in "the general Labor Pool" and that she and Rachel would have to live in a community residence. What do you think this means? Do you think this is a good solution for the unemployed? Why or why not? List the pros and cons for people in the following categories: Profession, Private Enterprise, Gainfully Employed, and Labor Pools. Which would you choose? Why?

3. What does Vivian mean when she says to Rachel, "I don't know that most governments really want to stop war—it has too many uses." Do you agree? Why or why not?

4. The National Border Defense System was supposed to provide safety for citizens of the Unified States. It also took away some freedoms. Do you think this system is a good idea? Why or why not?

5. Vivian refers to loss of freedoms and mistrust of friends and neighbors. Compare this to contemporary political climates around the world. How does the Unified States' economic system work? Are other world economic systems comparable? How? Make a list of the things in Rachel's world that require a lot of money (college, marriage, etc.). What kind of society is the government creating? What do you think is its ultimate goal? Is that goal right or wrong? Support your answers.

6. What do you think of the formal way in which Ms. Moore speaks while waiting for the doctor? What does this say about her character? How would you have reacted?

7. Reread the description of the furniture where Ms. Moore and Rachel have tea. What is Vivian's theory about why Ms. Moore still has the old-fashioned fireplace? What does this room reveal about Ms. Moore? Why does the author describe the chairs on either side of the fireplace as "friendly sentries"?

8. Did Rachel and Vivian do the right thing by not trying to help the woman and her child? Why or why

not? Although Rachel admits that she and her mother couldn't have stopped the woman and child involved in the Identification, "...she felt like they could have at least tried." What could Rachel and Vivian have done to help? What might you have done? Tell about a time when you wanted to help someone but didn't. Would you react differently now if you had the chance? Why or why not?

9. Rachel tells her mom that they are no better than the "monsters" in Ganivar who didn't help those taken away by the government. However, Rachel doesn't know the whole story. After reading Vivian's explanation, do you think Rachel should be told the rest of the story? Pretend to be Vivian's friend and advise her on what/how much to tell Rachel.

10. Rachel knows that "there were government agencies where people sat all day counting up hits on unapproved sites, flagging names for follow-up if they appeared too many times." Make a list of companies or groups who track people's Web use (online bookstores, grocery store cards, etc.). Why do they do this? How do you feel about it? Is it a good idea or not?

11. Using clues from the text, piece together what you think life is like for Pathik, his family, and his friends. Do you think the other people from Away live in similar conditions?

12. People often do dangerous things to help those they love. Is Pathik doing the right thing trying to contact a stranger on the other side of the Line?

13. Ms. Moore says that the Enforcement Officers have "power to simply haul people off if they want, with no formal charge." What other historical or current events does this mirror? Is this ever a good idea? Why or why not?

14. Ms. Moore says, "You can't be brave without being afraid. The brave ones are always afraid. But they do what they must, even so." Do you agree? Was Crossing the Line the right decision for Rachel? Will she regret her decision? Would you?

15. Elizabeth could have comforted Jonathan ". . . had she only told him the truth she was afraid to admit even to herself." What truth is she talking about? Think of a time when you've been reluctant to admit the truth even if it would have made someone feel better.

16. When Malgam was born, why didn't Elizabeth want his genid recorded? Why did the government start the genid program? If Malgam's father had not been one of the Others, would Elizabeth have let Dr. Beller record her baby's genid? List the pros and cons of genid recording. Would you be in favor of or opposed to a program like this? Explain your answer.

Turn the page for a preview of
Teri Hall's next novel:

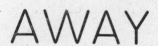

CHAPTER 1

"Awake, Rachel?" Pathik appeared, as he had for the last three mornings, holding two steaming cups of a bitter beverage the Others called root brew. He handed one to Rachel and sat down next to her. He looked weary, but he had looked that way for the whole of their short acquaintance.

She was *barely* awake, huddled on a crudely carved log that served as a bench, as close to the camp's central fire as she could get. During the six-day hike from the Line to Pathik's base camp, Rachel had begun to believe she would never be warm again. Though it was far from luxurious, the central fire pit had become one of her favorite places in camp.

She wrapped both hands around the dented metal cup and blew on the hot liquid, wishing for some kalitea, sweetened with sugar, served up in one of Ms. Moore's fine china cups. The cup she held now looked like it had been around for decades, yet it was one of the most modern things—at least of those still in one piece—that she had seen since she arrived Away. Everywhere she looked something mutely testified to the way time had just stopped here. The few buildings left standing were shells, with empty rooms and blown-out windows. There was no running water or heat. The lighting was provided by candles or oil. When the bombs went off all those years ago and Away was born, the activation of the Line cut off much more than a way back home for these people. It cut off any sort of access to technology. The forebears of the group that lived in this camp had had to figure out how to survive. Rachel was amazed they had managed it.

"Any change?" Rachel tried to read Pathik's expression for news of his father, Malgam. He was the reason she had Crossed the Line; he'd fallen ill and the camp healer couldn't help him. She'd helped Pathik bring medicine that the Others didn't have.

"Indigo said his fever broke last night. He's going to be okay, I think." Pathik spoke quietly; most of the camp's inhabitants were still sleeping.

Indigo was Pathik's grandfather, Malgam's father. Rachel had seen his face many times before she actually met him; Ms. Moore, the lady for whom Rachel's mother, Vivian, worked, had had a framed digim of him on her mantel. But the man in the digim was much younger looking, and his hair had been a rich brown color. Somehow, Rachel had expected Indigo to look just like the digim, though it had been taken many years before. When she first saw him on the night they arrived in camp, she was shocked at how his brown hair was now all silvery gray.

His eyes were the same, though—an intense, bottomless blue. When Indigo had looked at her the evening they arrived in camp, when he had thanked her for bringing the antibiotics Malgam needed, she felt like his eyes saw *inside* her. His smile shone through the worry she could see in his face and made her feel like he approved of her somehow.

"Do you know where my father is?" she had asked. She hadn't been able to help it, though she knew she should wait, knew that he needed to focus on his son.

"Your father?" He had tilted his head down at her, confused.

"She has a digim of Daniel." Pathik had whispered the words so the rest of the group gathered around the fire that night couldn't hear. "She showed it to me." He lowered his voice even more. "She says he's her father."

Indigo's eyes had widened then, but he hadn't answered her question.

"We will talk," he had said gently, "later." He had rushed away then, to tend to his son, but something lingered in her, some sense that he was an ally. It was a comforting balm in the midst of the confusion of that night—her first night in the Others' camp. She hadn't spoken to him again since then. She'd been waiting, catching glimpses of him as he went to tend to Malgam, but there had been no opportunity to speak to him.

"Morning, Jab." Pathik's voice brought Rachel back to the present, back to the chilly morning air and the smoke tendrilling toward her face. She looked up and saw Jab, one of the Others who had been with Pathik when he made his trek to the Line in search of medicine. He was holding his own cup of root brew, shivering.

"Have a seat." Pathik patted the log next to him. Jab glanced at Rachel and sat down.

"Morning," said Jab. He stared straight ahead at the fire.

Rachel was glad Pathik sat between them, though she knew that would provide no protection if Jab decided to use his gift again, like he had the day she Crossed. She remembered the pain, that hot flash in her temple, coming from nowhere. She and Pathik had just arrived at the temporary camp where Jab and Kinec, Pathik's trek companions, waited. Rachel had been shocked that she had actually Crossed, and was just beginning to realize that she might never be able to Cross back, that she might never see her mother again. But she hadn't yet thought to *fear* the Others, despite all the net books she had read about them, each filled with a more spectacular horror story than the last. When Pathik told her that Jab had caused the pain she felt, she realized that she knew nothing of them, not really. For the first time she had felt afraid of what the Others—even Pathik—might be capable of doing.

Rachel felt the faintest pang of that same fear when she saw Jab approach the fire. She knew that there had been a council meeting the night before to decide what punishment Jab would get for using his gift on her. It was forbidden for Others, at least the Others in Pathik's camp, to use their gifts without careful consideration.

"What's the verdict of the council?" Pathik didn't have to elaborate on his question; Jab knew what he meant.

"I'm to formally apologize." Jab kept his eyes on the campfire as he spoke. "To the camp and to her."

"That's all?" Pathik didn't sound pleased. "That's all they expect from you?"

Jab shrugged. "That and I'm to dredge all the common waste pots for the *entire* winter."

"Ha!" Pathik laughed. Emptying waste pots was drudgery. He was in charge of that chore for his household, so he knew it wasn't fun. But to have to do all the common pots, located throughout camp, for the entire winter? That would be a nightmare.

"Serves you right, Jab, and you know it."

Jab shrugged again. He leaned forward so he could see past Pathik, and waited until Rachel turned to look at him. "I do apologize," he said.

"Not good enough, Jab." Pathik's voice gained an edge.

Rachel knew that Pathik could tell whether Jab was sincere by using his gift; he could sense what others were feeling. *She* could tell without any gift at all that Jab didn't mean a word of his apology, but she didn't really care.

"It's fine," she said, turning away from Jab. She didn't want to prolong the interaction with him.

"Rachel." Pathik's voice was softer now. He waited for

her to look at him. When she did, he continued. "It's not fine. He hurt you." Pathik held her gaze for a moment, but then color infused his cheeks and he dropped his eyes. Rachel was glad he had looked down first; something in the look they exchanged had made her feel . . . *feelings;* feelings she didn't want to think about right now. She hoped Pathik wasn't aware of them; his gift might make that possible.

"A *formal* apology, Jab," said Pathik. "As the council decreed."

Jab groaned, but he stood up. He walked over and stood in front of Rachel, staring at her feet. She eyed him warily. He looked miserable.

"I am shamed by my actions." Jab hesitated. He heaved a huge sigh.

"I regret . . ." Pathik prompted.

"I *know*," hissed Jab, rolling his eyes. "I regret the harm I have caused. I apologize to you, Rachel Quillen. Will you name reparations?"

"Reparations?" Rachel crinkled her brow at Pathik. "What does that mean?"

"To provide compensation, to make amends, to—"

"Oh, I know what it means. What does it *mean*, though?" Rachel shook her head at Pathik's grin. Sometimes he could be exasperating.

"It means what it sounds like. You can ask Jab to do something, or even to give you something of his, to try and make up for what he did." Pathik grinned even wider at the look on Jab's face.

Rachel didn't think any of it was funny. "Can't I just say 'apology accepted' and leave it at that?"

Pathik quickly grew serious. "That's what usually happens, although there is a traditional way to say it. I think actually naming reparations was something that was done long ago. At least I don't remember anybody naming reparations recent—"

"What's the traditional response?" Normally, Rachel would have been fascinated by the details of how society functioned Away. At least she would have when she was still safe on The Property, like she had been less than two weeks ago. Right now, all she wanted was to get Jab out of her sight.

"We say: 'I ask only that you remember this and do better,'" said Pathik.

Rachel looked up at Jab. She knew she should just say the phrase and have done with it, but he looked so wretched. She tilted her head up at him, watching him through narrowed eyes. After what he'd done to her, she wanted his misery to last just a little while longer.

"Pathik. Rachel." Nandy called their names quietly from a few yards away. "You're both to come."

Pathik looked to be sure Rachel was coming and hurried to Nandy. When she saw the look on Pathik's face, Nandy immediately reassured him.

"All is well—Malgam's not worse. In fact, he was the one who sent for you."

"I couldn't tell," said Pathik. He hadn't tried to scan

Nandy for emotion; as all the Others did, he avoided using his gift on people he knew, unless he was practicing and had permission. But even without trying, he had felt something from her; her emotions were big lately, because Malgam had been so close to dying. Without focusing on her, he hadn't been able to tell if it was joy or anguish.

"I imagine he wants to have a look at this one." Nandy nodded at Rachel and smiled.

Rachel smiled back. She liked Nandy, had liked her right away, late that first night in camp. Nandy was close to Rachel's mother's age, though she didn't look like Vivian at all. Her hair was cut short and jagged, and her pale gray eyes were more frankly appraising than Vivian's. There was something about her that reminded Rachel of Vivian though, some maternal, protective quality. That first night, Nandy had been the one who finally told the rest of the camp that Rachel *had* to get some sleep. She had shushed all their urgent questions with a wave of her hand, and dismissed them.

It also didn't hurt that Nandy's name didn't mean anything.

Jab's name referred to his gift. Pathik's name too. But as far as Rachel could tell, Nandy just meant . . . *Nandy*. Which meant that Nandy probably didn't have a gift. No special power. Nothing for Rachel to fear. So it was easier to trust her.

The Others named their children after the gifts they developed, if they developed any. Pathik had explained to

Rachel that not all the Others developed gifts, so they kept their common names—the names they were given at birth. Nandy was a common name, and because she had never developed a gift, Nandy kept it as an adult. Even Indigo had never shown any signs of a special talent from what Rachel understood, and he had kept his common name, which was chosen because of the unusual color of his eyes.

Rachel thought most of the Others did develop something, even if it was nothing much. Kinec—the other boy who had been with Pathik and Jab when they made the trek to the Line—was named for his ability to move objects. He could make a fully loaded pack hop along the ground like a clumsy frog.

He had shown Rachel on the last night they spent together on their journey to Pathik's camp, just before they all wrapped up in the thermal blankets Ms. Moore had sent with them. The Others were taught not to show their gifts, but Pathik had said they could make an exception. And so, Kinec had placed his pack on the ground near the small campfire. He had stared at the pack intently, for so long that Rachel thought maybe nothing was going to happen. But then, the pack had lurched forward a few inches. Then it had actually leaped, not high, just half a foot off the ground, but it *left the ground*. It did that three times before Kinec grunted and collapsed.

"That's all I've got right now," he had said, beads of perspiration glittering on his brow.

Rachel was pretty sure Pathik had let Kinec show her his

gift to make her feel better, to let her know that not all gifts were about causing physical pain. But when she remembered that pack, jerking forward like a clumsy bullfrog brought back from the dead, somehow she wasn't comforted.

"Now remember, he's still not strong." Nandy stopped at the door of the largest building in camp, a one-story brick structure that was still in pretty good repair. Rachel had imagined many former uses for that building in the last few days: a beauty salon, or a flower shop that might have sold orchids like the ones Ms. Moore grew—the ones she had been learning to grow too, before she Crossed. She had settled on a bakery, probably because she had been hungry most of the last two weeks and it was appealing to make mental lists of all the different kinds of desserts the shop might have offered.

There were a couple of other, smaller buildings near the bakery building, remnants of a town that must have stood there years ago. Before the Line was activated. They were constructed of some sort of gray blocks. She had slept in one of them since she had arrived in camp, in a cramped room with another girl around her age, who said as little as possible to her. There was still pavement visible in front of one of the buildings, a sidewalk from a lost time, crumbled and cracked. It reminded Rachel of one of the stranger sights she had seen on their trek from the Line to the camp.